John Lyly's Galatea: A Retelling

David Bruce

Published by David Bruce, 2022.

JOHN LYLY'S GALATEA: A RETELLING

First edition. November 20, 2022.

Copyright © 2022 David Bruce.

ISBN: 979-8215357934

Written by David Bruce.

Table of Contents

Educate Yourself
Read Like A Wolf Eats
Be Excellent to Each Other
Books Then, Books Now, Books Forever

***

In this retelling, as in all my retellings, I have tried to make the work of literature accessible to modern readers who may lack the knowledge about mythology, religion, and history that the literary work's contemporary audience had.

Do you know a language other than English? If you do, I give you permission to translate this book, copyright your translation, publish or self-publish it, and keep all the royalties for yourself. (Do give me credit, of course, for the original retelling.)

I would like to see my retellings of classic literature used in schools, so I give permission to the country of Finland (and all other countries) to give copies of any or all of my retellings to all students forever. I also give permission to the state of Texas (and all other states) to give copies of any or all of my retellings to all students forever. I also give permission to all teachers to give copies of any or all of my retellings to all students forever. Of course, libraries are welcome to use my eBooks for free.

Teachers need not actually teach my retellings. Teachers are welcome to give students copies of my eBooks as background material. For example, if they are teaching Homer's *Iliad* and *Odyssey*, teachers are welcome to give students copies of my *Virgil's* Aeneid: *A Retelling in Prose* and tell them, "Here's another ancient epic you may want to read in your spare time."

CAST OF CHARACTERS

Tityrus, a shepherd

Galatea, his daughter, disguised as Tityrus II

Melebeus, a shepherd

Phillida, his daughter, disguised as Melebeus II

Venus, goddess of sexual passion

Cupid, god of affection and love, and son of Venus. Cupid is also known as Love.

Neptune, god of the sea

Diana, goddess of virginity and of the hunt

Telusa, a nymph of Diana

Eurota, a nymph of Diana

Ramia, a nymph of Diana

Larissa, a nymph of Diana

Another Nymph of Diana. Her name may be Servia or Clymene; they are mentioned in 3.1.

Ericthinis, another countryman of the shepherds

Hebe, his virgin daughter

An Augur

Rafe, son of a Miller, brother of Robin and Dick

Robin, son of a Miller, brother of Rafe and Dick

Dick, son of a Miller, brother of Rafe and Robin

A Mariner

An Alchemist

Peter, servant to an alchemist

An Astronomer

Fairies

Two countrymen of the shepherds

SCENE: A forest by the Humber River and adjacent woods. The Humber River is on the east coast of England.

NOTES:

Online Edition:

This is David Bevington's modern-spelling edition of the play (no notes included):

https://internetshakespeare.uvic.ca/doc/Gal_M/complete/index.html

Editions

Lyly, John. *Galatea*. Leah Scragg, editor. Revels Student Edition. Manchester and New York: Manchester University Press, 2012.

Lyly, John. *Galatea* and *Midas*. *Galatea* edited by George K. Hunter. *Midas* edited by David Bevington. The Revels Plays. New York: St. Martin's Press, 2000.

Lyly, John. *Gallathea and Midas*. Anne Begor Lancashire, editor. Lincoln, Nebraska: University of Nebraska Press, 1969.

Lyly, John. *The Plays of John Lyly*. Carter A. Daniel, editor. Lewisburg: Bucknell University Press. London and Toronto: Associated University Presses. 1988.

Lyly, John. *John Lyly: Selected Prose and Dramatic Work*. Leah Scragg, editor. Fyfield Books. Manchester: Carcanet, 1997.

Name of Main Character:

On 1 April 1585, printer Gabriel Cawood entered a play in the Stationers' Register under this title: *A Commoedie of Titirus and Galathea*.

The title page of the 1592 quarto uses this name: Gallathea.

Editor Leah Scragg uses the name "Gallathea" in her book *John Lyly: Selected Prose and Dramatic Work*.

But editor Leah Scragg uses the name "Galatea" in her book *Galatea*, a Revels Student Edition.

George K. Hunter uses the name "Galatea" in his edition of the play.

Astronomy

Copernicus (1473-1543) developed the heliocentric model that placed the sun at the center of the solar system and Galileo (1564-1642) championed Copernicus' work.

The first record of performance of *Galatea* is on New Year's Day of 1588, so Galileo was young. Astrology was still practiced: The astronomer in this play is very much an astrologer.

Language

In this society, a person of higher rank would use "thou," "thee," "thine," and "thy" when referring to a person of lower rank. (These terms were also used affectionately and between equals.) A person of lower rank would use "you" and "your" when referring to a person of higher rank.

The word "wench" at this time was not necessarily negative. It was often used affectionately.

The word "fair" can mean attractive, beautiful, handsome, good-looking.

"Sirrah" was a title used to address someone of a social rank inferior to the speaker. Friends, however, could use it to refer to each other, and fathers could call their sons "sirrah."

Love is nonrational. Suppose you are confronted with two individuals who are basically alike in beauty, form, character, and personality, but one individual is rich and the other individual is poor. Reason would tell you to fall in love with the rich individual, but you may fall in love with the poor individual.

In this book, "virgin" means "female virgin."

Natural "Facts"

Much of what Lyly says about nature and other societies is made up or are folk beliefs.

For example:

"The Egyptians never cut their dates from the tree, because they were so fresh and green; it is thought wickedness to pull roses from the stalks in the garden of Palestine, because they have so lively a red; and anyone who cuts the incense tree in Arabia before it falls commits sacrilege."

"[...] old eagles fly high into the air so the sun would heat them and open their pores so the eagles could shed their feathers. The eagles dived into water, which renewed their feathers and made the eagles young again."

PROLOGUE

The Prologue complimented Queen Elizabeth I:

"Ios and Smyrna were two sweet-smelling and fragrant cities. Ios was named after the violet, and Smyrna was named after the myrrh. Homer was born in Ios and buried in Smyrna.

"Your Majesty's judgment and favor are our sun and shadow. Your judgment comes from your deep wisdom, and your favor comes from your customary grace. We — the acting company — in all humility desire that by the former receiving our first breath, we may, in the latter, take our last rest.

"Augustus Caesar had such piercing eyes that whoever looked at him was constrained to close his eyes. Your Highness has so perfect a judgment that, whatsoever we offer, we are forced to blush.

"Yet as the Athenians were most careful that the lawn — fine linen — with which Minerva, goddess of wisdom, was covered should be without spot or wrinkle, so we have endeavored with all care to ensure that what we present Your Highness should neither offend in scene (actions) nor syllable (words) — knowing that as in the ground where gold grows and abounds, nothing will prosper but gold, so in Your Majesty's mind, where nothing harbors and resides except virtue, nothing can enter except virtue."

CHAPTER 1

— 1.1 —

Tityrus and Galatea sat under an oak tree. Tityrus was the father of Galatea, a young woman who was disguised as a boy. The name "Galatea" means "milk-white," and she was wearing a boy's white coat. They were on a bank of the Humber River.

"The sun beats upon the plain — the open — fields," Tityrus said. "Therefore, let us sit down, Galatea, under this fair oak tree, where being defended from the warm beams of the sun by the oak's broad leaves, we may enjoy the fresh air, which softly breathes from the Humber's water."

"Father, you have devised a good plan," Galatea said. "And while our flock of sheep roams up and down this pleasant green, you shall recount to me, if it pleases you, for what reason this tree was dedicated to Neptune, god of the sea, and why you have thus disguised me as a boy."

"I agree to tell you, and, when thy state and predicament and my care and concern are considered, thou shall know this request was not asked in vain," Tityrus said.

"I willingly listen to you," Galatea said.

Tityrus began:

"Where thou now see a heap of small pebbles, in times past stood a stately temple of white marble, which was dedicated to Neptune, the god of the sea, and properly so, because this location is so near the sea.

"Hither came all such as either ventured by long travel to see countries or by great traffic to engage in trade, offering sacrifice by fire to get safety by water, yielding thanks for past perils passed and making prayers for good success to come.

"But Lady Fortune, constant in nothing but inconstancy, changed her tone and her behavior as the people changed their customary practices; for, the land having been oppressed by Danes — who instead of sacrifice committed sacrilege, who instead of religion committed rebellion, and who made a prey of that in which they should have made their prayers, tearing down the temple, which was almost level with the skies, and making it level with the earth — so enraged the god who binds the winds in the hollows of the earth and creates storms at sea that he caused the seas to break their bounds since men had broken their vows, and to swell and flood as far above their usual reach and range as men had swerved beyond their reason."

The Danes often raided Britain, including British churches and monasteries, from 790 to 1069.

The god who binds the winds in the hollows of the earth is usually Aeolus, but here Neptune does that, perhaps in addition to Aeolus. Neptune and Aeolus both control storms at sea. Aeolus does that in Book 1 of Virgil's *Aeneid*, and then Neptune calms the winds and waves.

Tityrus continued:

"Then you might see ships sail where sheep fed, anchors cast where plows go, fishermen throw their nets where husbandmen — farmers — sow their grain, and fishes throw their scales where fowls breed their quills, aka feathers. Then you might gather froth where now is dew, gather rotten weeds instead of sweet roses, and you might see monstrous meremaids — mermaids — instead of surpassingly beautiful maids passing by."

A "mere" is an arm of the sea, or it is a lake or pond.

"To hear these sweet marvels, I wish my eyes were turned also into ears," Galatea said.

"But at last our countrymen repented, and not too late, because at last Neptune, either weary of his wrath or wary to do them wrong, consented to ease their miseries — upon condition," Tityrus said.

"What condition won't miserable men accept?" Galatea asked.

"The condition was this: that at a specified day observed every five years, the fairest and most chaste virgin in all the country should be brought to this tree, and here being bound (whom neither parentage shall excuse for honor, nor virtue and excellence for uncorrupted integrity), is left for a peace-offering to Neptune," Tityrus said.

Neither being born into a good family nor having uncorrupted virtue and integrity exempt a maiden from being a sacrifice to Neptune.

"Dear is the peace that is bought with guiltless blood," Galatea said.

"Dear" can mean 1) cherished, and 2) expensive. Galatea meant the second meaning, but in his answer Tityrus used the first meaning.

"I am not able to say that, but he sends a monster called the Agar, against whose coming the waters roar, the fowls fly away, and the cattle in the field shun the banks because of terror," Tityrus said.

Agar is a personification of "eagre," a tidal wave of unusual height created by the tide rushing up a narrow estuary. This is also called a tidal bore, or a bore.

"And is she bound to endure that horror?" Galatea asked.

By "bound," she meant "obliged."

"And she is bound to endure that horror," Tityrus answered.

By "bound," he meant "tied up."

"Does this monster devour her?" Galatea asked.

Tityrus said:

"Whether she is devoured by him, or conveyed to Neptune, or drowned between both, it is not permitted to know, and to conjecture what happens incurs danger to one's safety.

"Now, Galatea, here ends my tale and begins thy tragedy."

"Alas, father!" Galatea said. "And why so?"

Tityrus said:

"I wish that thou had been less beautiful or more fortunate. Then thou should not repine that I have disguised thee in this attire, for thy beauty will make thee to be thought worthy of this god.

"Therefore, to avoid destiny (for wisdom rules the stars and governs destiny), I think it better to use an unlawful means, with your honor preserved, than to endure intolerable grief, with both life and honor hazarded; and to prevent, if it should be possible, thy constellation — thy fate — by my crafty trick.

"Now thou have heard the custom of this country, the reason why this tree was dedicated to Neptune, and the vexing care and concern of thy fearful, apprehensive father."

Galatea said:

"Father, I have been attentive to hear, and with your patience and permission, I am ready to answer.

"Destiny may be deferred, not prevented; and therefore, it would be better to offer myself in triumph than to be forcibly drawn to it with dishonor."

A proverb stated, "It is impossible to avoid fate."

Galatea continued:

"Has nature (as you say) made me so beautiful above all others, and shall virtue not make me as famous as others?

"Don't you know, or does overcarefulness make you forget, that an honorable death is to be preferred before an infamous life? I am only a child, and I have not lived long, and yet I am not so childish that I desire to live forever.

"I intend to carry virtues to my grave, not gray hairs. I wish that I were as sure that destiny would alight and fall on me as I am resolved that it could not make me afraid.

"Nature has given me beauty, and virtue has given me courage. Nature must yield death to me, and virtue must yield honor to me. Permit me therefore to die, for which I was born, or let me curse that I was born, since I may not die for it."

A proverb stated, "He that [who] is once born must once die."

"Alas, Galatea, to consider the causes of change thou are too young, and that I should find them out for thee, thou are too, too fortunate," Tityrus said.

One kind of change was the change in Galatea's attire: her disguise. Another kind of change was going from youth to old age, as her father had done.

"The destiny to me cannot be as hard as the disguising is to me hateful," Galatea said.

She disliked wearing boys' clothing. She was resolved to be virtuous, and if being virtuous meant welcoming her fate, she would welcome it.

"To gain love, the gods have taken shapes of beasts, and to save life are thou too scrupulous and too reluctant to take the attire of men?" Tityrus said.

In one of his shape-shifting adventures, Jupiter, King of the gods, assumed the form of a swan and impregnated Leda, who gave birth both to Helen, who later became Helen of Troy, and to Clytemnestra, who married and later murdered Agamemnon, leader of the Greek forces against Troy.

"They were beastly gods, whom lust could make them appear as beasts," Galatea said.

She was right. The ancient Greeks and Romans were evil deceivers and rapists. Jupiter, King of the gods, was infamous for his unfaithfulness to his wife.

Tityrus said:

"In health it is easy to counsel the sick, but it's hard for the sick to follow wholesome counsel and good advice.

"Well, let us depart. The day is far spent."

They exited.

— 1.2 —

Cupid, the god of love, met a nymph who served Diana, the virgin goddess of hunting. Cupid carried a bow and arrows. If Cupid shoots a gold arrow into your heart, you fall in love.

"Fair nymph, have you strayed from your company by chance, or do you love to wander solitarily and on your own?" Cupid asked.

The nymph replied, "Fair boy, or god, or whatever you are, I would have you know that these woods are to me so well known that I cannot stray off my path even if I wanted to, and my mind is so free that I have no reason to be melancholy. There is none of Diana's train of followers whom anyone can train — that is, lure — either out of their way or out of their wits."

This society regarded wanting to be alone as a sign of melancholy.

Cupid asked, "Who is that Diana? A goddess? Who are her nymphs? Virgins? What are Diana's pastimes? Hunting?"

The nymph replied, "Is Diana a goddess? Who doesn't know it? Are her followers virgins? Who doesn't think it? Is Diana's favorite pastime hunting? Who doesn't love to hunt?"

"Please tell me, sweet wench, among all your sweet troop isn't there one who follows the sweetest thing, which is sweet love?" Cupid requested.

"Love, good sir?" the nymph said. "What do you mean by it? Or what do you call it?"

Cupid explained what love is:

"A heat full of coldness, a sweet full of bitterness, a pain full of pleasantness, which makes thoughts have eyes and makes hearts have ears, bred by desire, nursed by delight, weaned by jealousy, killed by dissembling, buried by ingratitude — this is love."

A proverb stated, "Love is a sweet torment."

Cupid then asked:

"Fair lady, will you have any? Do you want to try the experience of being in love?"

"If love is nothing else, then love is only a foolish thing," the nymph said.

"Try it, and you shall find it a pretty and pleasing thing," Cupid said.

The nymph said:

"I have neither the will nor the leisure — neither the desire nor the time — but I will follow Diana in the chase and the hunt, whose virgins are all chaste, delighting in the bow that wounds the swift hart in the forest, not fearing the bow that strikes the soft heart in the private chamber."

These are words that Cupid can — and will — take as a direct challenge. Cupid often makes people fall in love, even when they don't want to.

The nymph continued:

"This difference is between my mistress, Diana, and your mother, as I guess, Venus. All Diana's nymphs are amiable and friendly and wise in their kind — that is, by nature. In contrast, the other nymphs, those belonging to Venus, are amorous and too kind — that is, too affectionate — for their sex.

"And so farewell, little god."

Diana was the nymph's mistress: her female boss.

The nymph had guessed correctly that she had been talking to Cupid.

Cupid said to himself, "Diana, and thou, and all of thine shall know that Cupid is a great god. I will plot and scheme for a while — and for a wile, aka a trick — in these woods, and play such pranks with these nymphs that, while they aim to hit others with their arrows, they shall be wounded themselves with their own eyes."

A proverb stated, "Love comes by looking."

Cupid exited.

Melebeus and Phillida, his daughter, talked together. Phillida was the same age as Galatea, and like Galatea, she was beautiful. Unlike Galatea, Phillida was wearing feminine clothing.

Melebeus said:

"Come, Phillida, fair Phillida, and I fear that thou are too fair, thou being my Phillida, my daughter.

"Thou know the custom of this country, and I know the greatness of thy beauty; we both know the fierceness of the monster Agar. Everyone thinks his own child fair, but I know that which I most desire and would least have, that thou are the fairest.

"Thou shall therefore disguise thyself in boys' clothing, lest I should disguise myself in affection and act contrary to my love for you, my daughter, in allowing thee to perish by a fond — foolish, affectionate, doting — desire whom I may preserve by a sure and infallible deception."

The fathers of Galatea and Phillida were afraid that their daughters would be chosen as the sacrifice to Neptune, god of the sea.

Patriotism is love of one's country, but these fathers' love for their daughters came first.

Phillida said:

"Dear father, Nature could not make me as fair as she has made you kind and ready to act as a father ought to act, nor could Nature make you more kind than me dutiful. Whatever you command, I will not refuse to do because you command nothing but my safety and your happiness.

"But how shall I be disguised?"

"In man's apparel," Melebeus answered.

"It will suit neither my body nor my mind," Phillida objected.

"Why, Phillida?" Melebeus asked.

Phillida answered:

"For then I must keep company with boys and commit follies unseemly and inappropriate for my female sex. Or I must keep company with girls and be thought more wanton and unrestrained in behavior than becomes me.

"Besides, I shall be ashamed of my long hose and short coat — typical boys' clothing — and so unwarily blab out — that is, reveal — something by blushing at everything."

"Don't be afraid of that, Phillida," Melebeus said. "Use and custom will make it easy; fear must make it necessary."

Soon, Phillida will grow used to wearing men's clothing.

"I agree, since my father will have it so, and since fortune must have it so," Phillida said.

"Come, let us go in, and, when thou are disguised, we will roam about these woods until the time of the sacrifice has passed and Neptune is pleased," Melebeus said.

They exited.

— 1.4 —

A mariner, Rafe, Robin, and Dick talked together. They had been cast ashore in a shipwreck on the coast of Lincolnshire, near the mouth of the Humber River. Rafe, Robin, and Dick were brothers, and they were the sons of a miller.

"Now, mariner, what do thou call this sport and entertainment on the sea?" Robin asked.

"It is called a shipwreck," the mariner said.

"I take no pleasure in it," Rafe said. "Of all deaths, I would not be drowned. One's clothes will be so wet when he is taken up from out of the sea."

"What do thou call the thing we were bound to?" Dick asked.

"A rafter," the mariner said.

A rafter is a spar.

Rafe said:

"I will rather hang myself on a rafter — a beam — in the house than be so haled and pulled along in the sea; on a rafter in the house one may have a leap for his life.

"But I wonder how our shipmaster is doing."

Dick said:

"I'll warrant by this time he is wetshod and has wet feet. Did you ever see water bubble as the sea did?

"But what shall we do?"

"You are now in Lincolnshire, where you can lack no fowl, if you can devise means to catch them," the mariner said. "There are woods nearby, and there are houses a mile apart from each other, so that if you seek what you need on the land, you shall speed better and have more success than on the sea."

"Sea?" Robin said. "Nay, I will never sail anymore. I cannot endure or tolerate their diet. Their bread is so hard that one must carry a whetstone in his mouth to grind his teeth to sharpen them; the meat is so salty that one would think after dinner his tongue had been powdered with salt for ten days."

Whetstones are stones that are used to whet — sharpen — such tools as axes and knives.

In this society, liars were sometimes punished by having a heavy whetstone hung from their necks. Robin had done a fair amount of exaggerating.

Rafe said to the mariner:

"Oh, thou have a sweet life, mariner, to be pinned and confined within a few boards and planks, and to be within an inch of a thing bottomless."

Only one inch of planking on the ship's bottom lay between the sailors and the bottomless sea.

Rafe then said:

"I ask thee, how often have thou been drowned?"

"Fool, thou see I am still alive," the mariner said.

"Why, are they dead who are drowned?" Robin said. "I had thought they had been with the fish, and so by chance they had been caught up with them in a net again. It would be a shame if a little cold water should kill a man of reason, when you shall see a poor minnow lie in it that has no ability to understand or to reason."

The mariner said to Robin:

"Thou are wise from the crown of thy head upwards."

In other words: Thou are a fool. A wise man is wise from the crown — the top — of the head downwards.

He then said to the three brothers:

"Seek new fortunes now. I will follow my old fortune of being a sailor.

"I can shift the moon and the sun."

This sounds as if the mariner meant that he could move the moon and the sun, but he meant that he could record the variations in their positions.

The mariner continued:

"I know by one card what all of you cannot do and know by a whole pair. The loadstone — the magnet — that always holds his nose to the north, the two-and-thirty points for the wind, the wonders I see would make all you blind. You are just boys.

"I fear the sea no more than a dish of water. Why, fools, it is only a liquid element.

"Farewell."

In this society, a "whole pair" is a whole pack of cards. In this case, the mariner meant a pack of fortune-tellers' cards.

The one card the mariner has is a mariner's card, which has on it the thirty-two points of the compass.

The mariner turned and started to leave.

Robin said to his brothers, "It would be good for us if we learned his cunning at the cards, for we must live by cozenage and cheating. We have neither lands, nor wit, nor masters, nor honesty."

Robin was thinking about cheating at cards in order to make a living.

"Nay, I would like to have his thirty-two, that is, his three dozen lacking four points because you see that between us three there are not two good points," Rafe said.

"Points" are laces that connect the upper garments to hose, which are clothing for the legs: long stockings or breeches. Without points, the hose dropped.

Dick said:

"Let us call him back for a little while so that we may learn those points."

He then said to the mariner:

"Sirrah, a word. I ask thee to show us thy points."

The mariner, understanding "points" to mean the points on a compass, asked, "Will you learn?"

"Aye," Dick answered.

"Then as you like this, I will instruct you in all our secrets, for there is not a clout, nor card, nor board [ship's side], nor post [stem-post, from which the rudder is hung] that hasn't a special name or a singular and unique nature," the mariner said.

A "clout" is a sail.

"Well, begin with your points, for I lack only points in this world," Dick said.

Only points? He lacked everything, as he lacked all the 32 points of the mariner's card.

The mariner rattled off the points of one quadrant of a compass: "North. North and by east. North north-east. North-east and by north. North-east. North-east and by east. East north-east. East and by north. East —"

The mariner had named eight points and then Dick interrupted him as the mariner named another point, and so he had mentioned a quarter of the 32 points on the mariner's card.

Dick interrupted:

"— I'll say it. North. North-east. North-east. Nore-nore and by nore-east."

"Nore" means "nor," aka "north."

He paused to think, and then he said:

"I shall never do it."

"This is just one quarter," the mariner said.

A quarter is a quadrant.

Robin said:

"I shall never learn a quarter of it.

"I will try.

"North. North-east, is by the west side. North and by north."

"Surpassingly ill!" Dick said. "Very bad!"

The mariner asked Robin:

"Have thou no memory?"

He then said to Rafe:

"Thou try."

"North. North and by north," Rafe said. "I can go no further."

"O dullard! O fool!" the mariner said to Rafe. "Is thy head lighter than the wind, and is thy tongue so heavy that it will not wag and move? I will once again say it."

"I will never learn this language," Rafe said. "It will get only a small living — a small income — when it will hardly be learned until one is old."

The mariner said, "Then, farewell. And if your fortunes are not better than your wits and intelligence, you shall starve before you sleep."

He exited.

Rafe said:

"Was there ever such cozening and cheating?

"Come, let us go to the woods and see what fortune we may have before the woods are made into ships.

"As for our shipmaster, he is drowned."

"I will go this way," Dick said.

"I will go this way," Robin said.

"I will go this way, and on this date after a year has passed, let us all meet here again," Rafe said. "It may be we shall either beg together or hang together."

"It doesn't matter, as long as we are together," Dick said. "But let us sing now, even though we cry hereafter."

All three sang:

"Rocks, shelves, and sands, and seas, farewell!"

"Shelves" are sandbanks or submerged rock ledges.

All three continued to sing:

"*Fie! [Bah!] Who would dwell*

"*In such a hell*

"*As is a ship, which drunk does reel [reels like a drunk],*

"*Taking salt healths [Taking on sea water] from deck to keel.*"

Robin sang:

"*Up were we swallowed in wet graves,*"

Dick sang:

"*All soused [drenched] in waves,*"

Rafe sang:

"*By Neptune's slaves.*"

Neptune's slaves are wind and water, which he can command to make storms at sea.

All three sang:

"*What shall we do, being tossed to shore?*"

Robin sang:

"*Milk [Exploit] some blind tavern, and there roar.*"

A blind tavern is obscure, secret, private, or prone to being cheated.

"Roar" means "carouse and revel."

Rafe sang:

"*'Tis [It is] brave [splendid], my boys, to sail on land,*

"*For being well manned,*

"*We can cry 'Stand!'*"

"Well manned" can mean 1) well supplied with men, or 2) well hung.

The full highwayman's command is "Stand and deliver!" It means, "Stand still and deliver — hand over — your valuables."

In Elizabethan slang, the word "stand" also means "erection."

Dick sang:

"*The trade of pursing [stealing purses, aka bags of money] ne'er shall fail*

"*Until the hangman cries, 'Strike sail!'*"

When a ship surrenders, it strikes — lowers — its sails. It also lowers its sails when a voyage reaches its destination.

Here, the hangman is ordering someone to surrender his life. The person's life has reached its end.

All sang:

"*Rove [Roam], then, no matter whither,*

"*In fair or stormy weather.*

"*And as we live, let's die together.*

"*One hempen caper cuts a feather.*"

One kind of "hempen caper" is dancing at the end of a hangman's noose while suspended in air.

"Caper" also means "privateer." "Hempen" is clothing made of hemp. Another meaning of "hempen caper" is a privateer wearing hempen clothing.

"Cuts a feather" means "making fine distinctions." The jerk of a hangman's noose makes a distinction between life and death.

"Cuts a feather" also means "making foam at the front end of a ship."

Erotic asphyxiation occurs when a person hangs until he ejaculates. A hanged man who dangles for a while, still alive, can ejaculate. The semen can be compared to foam. When a person does this intentionally, it is called auto-erotic asphyxiation.

The three brothers' meaning is "Let's die together because our group will be broken up if only one of us hangs."

They exited.

CHAPTER 2
— 2.1 —

Alone, the disguised-as-a-boy Galatea said to herself:

"Blush, Galatea, you who must frame thy affection fit for thy habit — thy male clothing — and therefore be thought immodest because thou are unfortunate!"

She had to make her thoughts fit with her clothing; that is, she had to begin thinking like a boy. If people knew that she was dressed as a boy, they would look down on her.

Galatea continued:

"Thy young, tender years cannot dissemble this deceit, nor thy sex bear it.

"Oh, I wish that the gods had made me as I seem to be (a boy), or that I might safely be what I seem not to be (a girl)!

"Thy father dotes, Galatea, whose blind love corrupts his fond judgment, and, apprehensive and fearful about thy death, seems to dote on thy beauty; whose fond — foolish but loving — care and concern carry his partial eye as far from truth as his heart is from falsehood."

Galatea's father loved her, and he was afraid that she could become a sacrifice to Neptune and die. This fear made him a little insane, according to her, and so he had made her dress in boys' clothing, something that Galatea did not want to do. His heart was filled with love for her, but his worry about her was affecting his judgment, according to her.

Galatea continued:

"But why do thou blame him, or blab and reveal what thou are, when thou should only counterfeit and pretend to be what thou are not?

"But whist — hush! Here comes a lad. I will learn from him how to behave and conduct myself as a boy."

She stood aside, not readily noticeable.

Phillida, wearing men's clothing, entered the scene. She was practicing walking like a boy.

Phillida said to herself, "I like neither my gait nor my garments: The one is untoward and awkward, the other is unfit, and both are unseemly."

By "unfit" and "unseemly," Phillida meant unfit and unseemly for a girl.

She continued:

"O Phillida! But yonder stands someone, and therefore I will say nothing. But O Phillida!"

While looking at and listening to the disguised Phillida, the disguised Galatea said to herself, "I perceive that boys are in as great disliking of themselves as maidens. Therefore, although I wear the apparel, I am glad I am not the person."

The disguised Phillida said to herself, "He is a pretty boy and a handsome boy. He might well have been a woman, but because he is not, I am glad I am, for now, under the color — the disguise — of my boys' coat and outfit, I shall decipher the follies of their sex."

While looking at the disguised Phillida, the disguised Galatea said to herself, "I would greet him, but I fear that I would make a woman's curtsy instead of a man's bow."

Phillida said to herself, "If I dared to trust my face as well as I do my clothing, I would spend some time to make pastime and have some entertainment; for, say what they will of a man's wit and intelligence, it is no second thing to be a woman — women are not inferior to men."

Galatea said to herself, "All the blood in my body would be in my face, if he would ask me (as the question among men is common), 'Are you a maiden? Are you a virgin?'"

Phillida said to herself, "Why do I stand still? Boys should be bold. But here comes a brave and splendid train of people who will spill — will ruin — all our talk."

The goddess Diana and two of her nymphs, Telusa and Eurota, entered the scene. They were hunting.

Diana said to the disguised Galatea, "God speed, fair boy. May God make you prosper."

"You are deceived, lady," Galatea said, hearing the word "boy" and speaking without thinking.

"Why, are you no boy?" Diana asked.

Recovering her wits, Galatea said, "I am no *fair* boy."

"But I see an unhappy boy," Diana said.

Telusa asked the disguised Galatea, "Didn't you see the deer come this way? He flew away in the direction the wind was blowing to prevent us from following his scent, and I believe you have blanched him — I believe that you have made him turn back in fright."

"Whose deer was it, lady?" the disguised Galatea asked.

"Diana's deer," Telusa said.

"I saw none but my own dear," the disguised Galatea said.

Galatea was already in love with the disguised Phillida.

Telusa said to Diana, "This mischievous wag is wanton — is perverse, or is joking — or is a fool! Ask the other boy, Diana."

The disguised Galatea said to herself, "I don't know how it comes to pass, but yonder boy is in my eye too beautiful. I pray to the gods that the ladies won't think him their dear!"

Diana asked the disguised Phillida, "Pretty lad, do your sheep feed in the forest, or have you strayed from your flock, or do you come on purpose to mar Diana's pastime?"

"I don't understand one word that you speak," the disguised Phillida replied.

"What, are thou neither lad nor shepherd?" Diana asked.

The disguised Phillida answered, "My mother said I could be no lad until I was twenty years old, nor keep sheep until I could tell — count — them; and therefore, lady, neither lad nor shepherd is here."

In pastoral poetry, a "lad" is a young shepherd. In 1599, eleven years after scholars think *Galatea* was first performed, Christopher Marlowe's poem "The Passionate Shepherd to His Love," whose first line is "Come live with me and be my love," was first published.

Phillida's mother wanted her to be grown up before she married.

According to the *Oxford English Dictionary*, a "lad" can also be a spirited man, or, colloquially, a spirited girl.

A proverb stated, "If you cannot tell, you are nought to keep sheep."

Telusa said to Diana, "These boys are both alike. Either they are very pleasant and merry, or they are too perverse. You would do best, lady, to make them tusk these woods, while we stand by with our bows, and so use them as hunting beagles since they have so good mouths."

"Tusk the woods" means to beat the woods and make a lot of noise so that the deer will flee in the direction of the hunters.

"Good mouths" means 1) good at barking, or 2) good at talking.

Diana said:

"I will."

She then said to Phillida:

"Follow me without delay or excuse, and, if you can do nothing, yet you shall halloo the deer and pursue them with shouts."

Phillida said out loud:

"I am willing to go —"

She then continued, saying to herself, "— not for these ladies' company, because I myself am a virgin girl, but for that fair boy's favor, who I think is a god."

"Favor" means 1) appearance, and 2) goodwill.

Diana said to the disguised Galatea, "You, sir boy, shall also go."

Galatea said out loud:

"I must go if you command —"

She then continued, saying to herself, "— and I would go if you had not."

They exited.

Cupid, wearing the clothing of a nymph, thought he was alone, but Neptune was nearby, listening.

He said to himself:

"Now, Cupid, under the disguise of a silly, foolish girl, show the power of a mighty god. Let Diana and all her coy, disdainful nymphs know that there is no heart so chaste but thy bow can wound it, nor eyes so modest but thy firebrands — thy torches — can kindle them, nor thoughts so staid [sober] and stayed [unwavering] but thy shafts can make them wavering, weak, and wanton.

"Cupid, although he is — I am — a child, is no baby. I will make their pains my pastimes and pleasures, and I will so confound their loves by making them love people of their own so that they shall go mad in their desires, delight in their affections and passions, and practice only impossibilities.

"While I am truant from my mother, Venus, the goddess of sexual passion, I will practice some tyranny in these woods, and their exercise in foolish love shall be my excuse for running away.

"I will see whether fair faces are always chaste, and whether Diana's virgins are uniquely and preeminently modest; or else I will expend both my shafts and shifts — I will exhaust all my arrows and all my wily tricks."

Cupid then directly addressed the women reading this book:

"And then, ladies, if you see these dainty dames entrapped in love, say softly to yourselves, we may all love."

Cupid exited.

Neptune stepped forward and said to himself:

"Do silly, foolish shepherds go about to deceive great Neptune by putting men's clothing on women, and does Cupid, to make entertainment, deceive them all by putting a woman's apparel on a god: himself?

"Then, Neptune, I who have taken various shapes to obtain love, don't hesitate to practice some deceit to show thy deity, and, having often thrust thyself into the shape of beasts to deceive men, don't be reluctant to adopt the shape of a shepherd to show thyself a god."

Neptune became a horse to sleep with Ceres. (Her Greek name is Demeter.) He pursued her, but she did not want to be pursued, so she turned herself into a mare. The trick didn't work because Neptune turned himself into a stallion. Their offspring was Arion, a horse that saved the life of Adrastus, King of Argos, during the War of the Seven Against Thebes.

Neptune became a ram to sleep with Theophane. She was so beautiful that many would-be lovers pursued her. Neptune carried her to the island of Crinissa. The would-be lovers pursued her even there, so Neptune turned Theophane into an ewe and himself into a ram. Their offspring was the ram with the golden fleece of Jason and the Argonauts fame.

Neptune became a steer to sleep with Arne. Her mother had been transformed into a mare, and so Arne was born a colt, but she later gained human form. While in the form of a bull, Neptune fathered Aeolus and Boeotia with her.

Neptune continued:

"Neptune cannot be overreached — be outwitted — by swains: lovers. He himself is subtle and cunning, and, if Diana will be overtaken by craft, then Cupid is wise."

He did not think that Diana could be taken in by a trick, and he did not think that Cupid was wise.

Neptune continued:

"I will go into these woods and closely observe all that happens, and in the end, I will mar all."

Alone, Rafe said to himself:

"Do you call this the seeking of fortunes, when one can find nothing but birds' nests? I wish that I were out of these woods! For I shall have only wooden luck here."

"Wooden luck" is much different from "golden luck."

If something is "wooden," it is dull, worthless, inferior.

Rafe continued:

"Here's nothing but the shrieking of ill-omened owls, croaking of frogs, hissing of adders, barking of foxes, and walking of hags, aka witches or evil spirits in female form.

"But what are these?"

Some fairies entered the scene. They danced and played on musical instruments, and then they exited.

Rafe said:

"I will follow them. To hell I shall not go, for such fair faces never can have such hard fortunes."

Of course, some virgins with fair faces were sacrificed to get Neptune's favor.

Seeing someone approaching, Rafe said:

"What black boy is this?"

"Black" can mean 1) covered with soot and dirt, and/or 2) having black hair or a dark complexion.

The alchemist's serving-boy, Peter, entered the scene.

Thinking that he was alone, Peter said to himself:

"What a life do I lead with my master! Nothing but the blowing of bellows, the beating of spirits, and the scraping of crosslets, aka crucibles."

"Spirits" are four liquid essences used by alchemists.

Peter continued:

"It is a very secret science, for almost no one can understand the language of it: sublimation, almigation, calcination, rubification, incorporation, circination, cementation, albification, and fermentation, with as many terms unpossible and impossible to be uttered as the art to be encompassed and mastered."

Rafe did not know these alchemical terms, and you, the readers, don't need to know them, unless you have a need to learn alchemical jargon.

Actually, Peter did not entirely know these terms, either. "Almigation" should be "amalgamation."

Rafe said to himself, "Let me cross myself. I never heard so many great devils in a little monkey's mouth."

He thought that Peter was saying the names of devils.

Peter then said to himself, "Then our instruments: crosslets, sublimatories, cucurbits, limbecks, decensors, vials, manual and mural, for imbibing and conbibing, bellows molificative and indurative."

Rafe did not know these alchemical terms, and you, the readers, don't need to know them, unless you have a need to learn alchemical jargon.

Rafe said to himself, "What language is this? Do they — do devils — speak so?"

Peter then said to himself, "Then our metals: saltpeter, vitriol, sal tartar, sal preparat, argoll, resagar, sal ammoniac, agrimony, lunary, brimstone, valerian, tartar alum, breemwort, glass, unslaked lime, chalk, ashes, hair, and what not, to make I don't know what."

An obsolete meaning of "metal" is "Material, matter, substance, fabric," according to the *Oxford English Dictionary*.

Rafe did not know these alchemical terms, and you, the readers, don't need to know them, unless you have a need to learn alchemical jargon.

So how did John Lyly know them? He read Reginald Scot's *Discoverie of Witchcrafte* (1584) and Chaucer's "Canon's Yeoman's Tale" from *The Canterbury Tales*.

Rafe said to himself, "My hair begins to stand upright. I wish that the boy would make an end!"

Peter said to himself, "And yet such a beggarly science it is, and so strong on multiplication that the end is to have neither gold, nor wit, nor honesty."

"Multiplication" is "making much out of little."

Rafe said to himself:

"Then I am just of thy occupation."

He stepped forward and said:

"What! Fellow, we are well met!"

Peter said, "Are we fellows? Upon what acquaintance?"

Fellows have something in common.

Rafe said, "Why, thou say the end of thy occupation is to have neither wit, nor money, nor honesty; and I think, at a blush — that is, at first glance — thou should be one of my occupation."

"Thou are deceived," Peter said. "My master is an alchemist."

"What's that?" Rafe said. "A man?"

Peter said:

"A little more than a man, and a hair's breadth less than a god. He can make thy cap gold, and, by multiplication of one groat, he can make three old angels."

A groat is a silver coin of little value. Angels are gold coins of much greater value than a groat.

During 1544-1551, the Great Debasement occurred under King Henry VIII. The amount of gold and silver in gold and silver was lowered.

According to Peter, the alchemist could take a little of something of value and turn it into a lot of something of value. The alchemist could take a little silver and turn it into much gold.

Peter continued:

"I have known him from the metal tag of a point to make a silver bowl of a pint."

Points are laces with metal tags on each end.

According to Peter, the alchemist he serves can take a small metal tag and make from it a silver bowl that can hold one pint.

Alchemists tried to make much out of little. Their main goal was the creation of the philosopher's stone, which could be used to turn lead into gold. The philosopher's stone does not exist, and many alchemists were conmen who tried to convince suckers to give them money to buy expensive materials that they said they would use to create the philosopher's stone. Alchemists are punished in the tenth ditch of the eighth circle of Dante's *Inferno*. Alchemists tried to turn lead into gold, and in the *Inferno*, their healthy skin is changed into diseased skin. They have leprosy, which is fitting because sin is a kind of disease.

Rafe said:

"That makes thee have never a point; they are all turned into pots."

Apparently, Peter the apprentice was like Rafe: lacking points to hold up his hose.

Rafe continued:

"But if he can do this, he shall be a god altogether."

Peter said, "If thou have any gold to work on, thou are then made forever, for with one pound of gold he will go near to — that is, almost — pave ten acres of ground."

"How might a man serve him and learn his cunning skill?" Rafe asked.

Peter said:

"Easily.

"First, seem to understand the terms, and especially note and remember these points:

"In our art there are four spirits."

"Nay, I have done, if you work with devils!" Rafe said.

Peter said:

"Thou are gross and thick-witted.

"We call 'spirits' those things that are the grounds — the foundation — of our art, and, as it were, the metals more incorporative [capable of combining] for domination over other substances.

"The first spirit is quicksilver."

"That is my spirit, for my silver is so quick that I have much ado and trouble to catch it; and when I have it, it is so nimble that I cannot hold it," Rafe said. "I thought there was a devil in it."

"The second spirit is *orpiment*," Peter said.

"That's no spirit, but a word to conjure a spirit," Rafe said.

To conjure a spirit, one may *compliment* the spirit by recognizing what they are princes and monarchs of, as Christopher Marlowe's Doctor Faustus did when he said these Latin words:

"*Sint mihi dei Acherontis propitii! Valeat numen triplex Jehovae! Ignei, aerii, aquatici spiritus, salvete! Orientis Princeps Belzebub, inferni ardentis monarcha, et Demogorgon, propitiamus vos, ut appareat et surgat Mephastophilis. Quod tu moraris. Per Jehovam, Gehennam, et consecratam aquam quam nunc spargo, signumque crucis quod nunc facio, et per vota nostra, ipse nunc surgat nobis dicatus Mephastophilis!*"

Translated, the Latin passage means this:

"May the gods of Acheron be favorable to me! Farewell to the threefold spirit of Jehovah — the Trinity! Welcome, you spirits of fire, air, and water! Prince of the East; Belzebub, monarch of burning Hell; and Demogorgon, we ask that Mephastophilis may appear and rise."

The word "orp" means "nag," however, so if the compliments don't work, nagging at the spirits might work. Or one of the other meanings of "orp" may apply to spirit-summoning.

According to the *Oxford English Dictionary*, "orp" means, "To fret, to murmur discontentedly, to complain, to nag." The first entry, however, is dated 1634.

But the first entry for the adjective "orpit," meaning "Fretful, discontented," is 1525.

"The third spirit is sal ammoniac," Peter said.

"A proper word," Rafe said.

He may have been thinking of "demoniac."

"The fourth spirit is brimstone," Peter said.

Rafe said:

"That's a stinking spirit. I thought there was some spirit in it because it burnt so blue."

Brimstone is sulphur. When burned, it stinks and it produces a blue flame.

Rafe continued:

"For my mother would often tell me that when the candle burnt blue, there was some ill spirit in the house, and now I perceive it was the spirit brimstone."

"Thou can remember these four spirits?" Peter asked.

"Let me alone — leave it to me — to conjure them," Rafe said.

Peter said:

"Now there are also seven bodies —"

The seven bodies are the seven metals known to the ancients: copper, gold, iron, lead, mercury, silver, and tin.

Peter then said:

"— but here comes my master."

The alchemist, who was poorly dressed, entered the scene and stood apart from Rafe and Peter.

"This is a beggar," Rafe said.

"No," Peter said. "Such cunning, wise men must disguise themselves as though there were nothing — no special knowledge — in them, for otherwise they shall be compelled to work for princes, and so be constrained and forced to betray and reveal their secrets."

"I don't like his attire, but I am enamored of his art," Rafe said.

The alchemist said to himself, "An ounce of silver limed, as much of crude mercury, of spirits four, being tempered with the bodies seven, by multiplying of it ten times, comes for one pound eight thousand pounds, provided that I may have only beechen coals: coals made from burning beechwood."

The alchemist was possibly talking about turning one pound of silver into eight thousand pounds — if only he could get the right materials.

Perhaps the alchemist had wanted to be overheard.

"Is it possible?" asked Rafe, who had overheard the alchemist.

"It is more certain than certainty," Peter said.

"I'll tell thee one secret: I stole a silver thimble," Rafe said. "Do thou think that he will make it a pottle pot: a two-quart pot?"

Peter said:

"A pottle pot? Nay, I dare assure thou that he will make it a whole cupboard of silver-plated dishes. Why, from the quintessence of a leaden plummet — a sinker on a fishing line — he has made twenty dozen silver spoons.

"Look at him. Look at how he studies and thinks in his mind. I dare to bet my life that he is now casting about and considering how he may make golden bracelets from his breath, for often he has made silver drops — silver earrings or silver pendants — from smoke."

"What do I hear?" Rafe asked, incredulous. "What are you telling me?"

"Did thou never hear how Jupiter came in a golden shower to Danae?" Peter asked.

"I remember that tale," Rafe said.

Jupiter lusted after the mortal maiden Danae. The gods are shape-shifters, and Jupiter assumed the form of a shower of gold, passed through the roof of her prison and impregnated her. She gave birth to the hero Perseus.

Peter said:

"That shower my master made from a spoonful of tartar alum, but with the fire of blood and the corrosive acid of the air, he is able to make nothing infinite."

No, the alchemist cannot make an infinite amount of something out of nothing.

Yes, the alchemist is able to make an infinite amount of nothing out of nothing.

Peter continued:

"But whist — hush! He sees us."

The alchemist came forward and asked, "What! Peter, do you loiter, knowing that every minute increases our mine: our hoard?"

"I was glad to take air, for the metal came so fast that I feared my face would have been turned to silver," Peter said.

Alchemist pointed to Rafe and asked, "But what stripling is this?"

"One who is desirous to learn your craft," Peter said.

"Craft, sir boy?" the alchemist said. "You must call it a mystery."

A craft is a trade. A mystery is a craft that involves much secrecy.

"All is one," Rafe said. "It is the same thing: a crafty mystery, and a mystical craft."

"Can thou take pains?" the alchemist asked.

"Take pains" can mean 1) be conscientious, or 2) endure suffering.

"Infinite," Rafe said.

"But thou must be sworn to be secret, and then I will entertain — hire — thee," the alchemist said.

By "be sworn," the alchemist meant for Rafe to take an oath not to reveal alchemical secrets.

Rafe, who understood "swear" to mean "utter profanity," said, "Although I am a poor fellow, I can swear as well as the best man in the shire. But, sir, I much marvel that you, being so cunning, should be so ragged."

The alchemist said:

"O my child, gryphs — griffins, which are part eagle and part lion — make their nests of gold, although their coats are feathers, and we feather our nests and enrich ourselves with diamonds, although our garments are made only of coarse woolen frieze.

"If thou knew the secret of this science, the cunning knowledge would make thee so proud that thou would disdain the outward pomp."

Peter said to Rafe, "My master is so ravished with his art that we many times go supperless to bed, for he will make gold of his bread, and such is the drought of his desire that we all wish our very guts were gold."

The "drought of his desire" is the lack of what he desires: food.

If their guts were made of gold and not of living flesh, they would not feel hunger.

"I have good fortune to alight upon such a master," Rafe said.

The alchemist said, "When in the depth of my skill, I determine to try the uttermost of my art, I am dissuaded by the gods. Otherwise, I would dare to undertake to make the fire, as it flames, gold; the wind, as it blows, silver; the water, as it runs, lead; the earth, as it stands, iron; the sky, brass; and men's thoughts, firm metals and mettles."

"I must bless myself, and I must marvel at you," Rafe said.

"Come in, and thou shall see all," the alchemist said.

The alchemist exited.

"I follow, I run, I fly," Rafe said. "They say my father has a golden thumb. You shall see me have a golden body."

A proverb stated, "An honest miller has a golden thumb."

Possibly, the proverb means that honest millers are as rare as golden thumbs.

But possibly, if the proverb is "An 'honest' miller has a golden thumb," then the miller keeps his thumb on the scale when measuring meal.

Chaucer wrote about the miller in *The Canterbury Tales*, "And yet he hadde a thombe of gold, pardee."

Also possibly, a golden thumb may be a useful thumb. Possibly, Rafe's father, a miller, rubbed meal between his thumb and index finger to test its quality. Because he was skillful as a miller, he could make his living honestly without resorting to put his thumb on the scale.

Rafe exited.

Alone, Peter said to himself:

"I am glad of this, for now I shall have leisure to run away. Alchemy is such a bald — paltry and unproductive — art as never was!

"Let the alchemist keep his new serving-man, for he shall never see his old serving-man again. May God shield and protect me from blowing gold to nothing, with a strong imagination to make nothing anything!

"Blowing gold to nothing" means to spend labor and materials on an activity that yields nothing of value.

Fairies can be malicious or benevolent, and so can people.

The fairies had danced and sang; providing good entertainment is benevolent.

Peter had done much lying in order to get Rafe to become the alchemist's new serving-man, and that was malicious.

— 2.4 —

Alone, the disguised Galatea said to herself:

"How are you now, Galatea?

"Miserable Galatea, who, having put on the apparel of a boy, thou cannot also put on the mind of a boy.

"O fair Melebeus!"

This Melebeus was the disguised Phillida, who had taken her father's name. Galatea had also adopted her father's name: Tityrus.

Galatea continued:

"Aye, too fair, and therefore, I fear, too proud."

Galatea said about herself:

"Wouldn't it have been better for thee to have been a sacrifice to Neptune than a slave to Cupid? To die for thy country than to live in thy fancy? To be a sacrifice than a lover?

"Oh, I wish that when I hunted his — Melebeus' — eye with my heart, he might have seen my heart with his eyes!

"Why did Nature to him, a boy, give a face so fair, and why did Nature to me, a virgin, give a fortune so hard?

"I will now use for the distaff the bow and play at quoits abroad — out of doors — I who was accustomed to sew in my sampler at home."

A distaff is used in spinning thread, typically designated as women's work.

Quoits is a game similar to horseshoes.

A sampler is a piece of embroidery that illustrates the embroiderer's skill.

She continued:

"It may be, Galatea —

"— foolish Galatea, what may be? Nothing.

"Let me follow him into the woods, and thou, sweet Venus, be my guide!"

— 2.5 —

Alone, the disguised Phillida said to herself:

"Poor Phillida, curse the time of thy birth and the splendidness of thy beauty, the inappropriateness of thy apparel, and the untamedness of thy affections and desires.

"Are thou no sooner in the clothing of a boy but thou must be enamored of and in love with a boy?

"What shall thou do when what best pleases thee also most discontents thee?

"Go into the woods, watch the good times, watch his best moods, and transgress in love a little of thy modesty.

"I will … I dare not.

"Thou must … I cannot.

"Then pine in thine own peevishness and foolishness.

"I will not … I will.

"Ah, Phillida, do something, nay, anything, rather than live thus! Well, what I will do, I myself don't know, but what I ought to do — suppress my feelings of love — I know too well. And so I go, resolute either to betray and reveal my love or to suffer shame."

The shame would be not to pursue the one she loved.

She exited.

CHAPTER 3
— 3.1 —

Alone, the nymph Telusa said to herself:

"What is this now?

"What new conceits and ideas and fancies, what strange contraries, breed in thy mind? Has thy Diana become a Venus, have thy chaste thoughts turned into wanton looks, has thy conquering modesty turned into a captive and enthralled imagination?"

She was asking herself if she now worshipped Venus, sexually active goddess of sexual passion, instead of Diana, virgin goddess of the hunt.

Telusa continued:

"Do thou begin with piralis to die in the air and live in the fire, to leave the sweet delight of hunting and to follow the hot desire of love?"

A piralis is a mythological bird that lives in fire and languishes out of it.

Telusa continued:

"O Telusa, these words are unfit for thy sex, you being a female virgin, but they are apt for thy affections and passions, you being a lover. And can there in years so young, in education so strict, in vows so holy, and in a heart so chaste, enter either a strong desire or a wish or a wavering thought of love?

"Can Cupid's firebrands — his torches — quench the flames of Vesta, the goddess of the hearth, and can Cupid's feeble shafts headed with feathers pierce deeper than Diana's arrows headed with steel?"

Vesta's flames were supposed to be kept burning eternally in her temple. Vesta and her female devotees who tended the eternal fire were virgins. In fact, her female devotees were known as Vestal Virgins.

Telusa continued:

"Break thy bow, Telusa, you who seek to break thy vow, and let those hands that aimed to hit the wild hart — wild deer — scratch out those eyes that have wounded thy tame heart.

"O vain and wholly empty and naked name of chastity, which is made out to be eternal and perishes by time, which is made out to be holy and is infected by fancy, and which is made out to be divine and is made mortal by folly!

"Virgins' hearts, I perceive, are not unlike cotton trees, whose fruit is so hard in the bud that it resounds like steel, and, being ripe, pours forth nothing but wool; and virgins' thoughts are like the leaves of lunary, which, the further they grow from the sun, the sooner they are scorched with his beams."

Lunary is a plant also known as moonwort, which flourishes in the shade and dies in hot, direct sunshine.

Virgins' hearts may receive protection (may be hard and distant), but still they eventually will become soft and yielding.

In other words: Virgins will eventually fall in love.

Telusa continued:

"O Melebeus, because thou are fair, must I be fickle and violate my vow of chastity because I see thy virtue? Fond, foolish girl whom I am, to think of love! Nay, it is a vain profession and vocation that I follow, to disdain love!

"But here comes Eurota. I must now put on a red mask and blush, lest she perceive my pale face and laugh."

She needed to pretend to have a red face from the exertions of hunting.

Eurota entered the scene.

She said:

"Telusa, Diana told me to hunt you out, and she said that you don't care to hunt with her; but if you follow any other game than the game she has roused to be hunted, your punishment shall be to bend all our bows and weave all our bowstrings: You shall string all our bows."

Bowstrings were made of hemp, flax, or silk. Individual strings were twisted or woven together to form a bowstring.

Eurota then asked:

"Why do you look so pale, so sad, so wildly?"

"Eurota, the game I follow is the thing I flee," Telusa said. "My strange disease is my chief desire."

Eurota said:

"I am no Oedipus to expound riddles, and I muse how thou can be Sphinx to utter them."

The Sphinx is a mythological creature with the head of a human and the body of a lion. In Sophocles' tragedy *Oedipus Rex*, the Sphinx, which has the head of a woman, asks Oedipus this riddle: What goes on four legs in the morning, two legs at noon, and three legs in the evening? If Oedipus cannot answer this riddle correctly, the Sphinx will kill him. Fortunately, Oedipus does answer the riddle correctly: Man, who goes on hands and knees as a crawling baby, two legs as a healthy adult, and two legs and a cane as an old person.

Eurota continued:

"But I ask thee, Telusa, to tell me what ails thou. What is wrong?

"If thou are sick, this ground has leaves to heal thee.

"If thou are melancholy, here are pastimes to use to divert yourself.

"If thou are peevish and foolish, wit must wean it, or time, or counsel.

"If thou are in love (for I have heard of such a beast called Love), it shall be cured."

"Wit must wean it" means that intelligence must cure you of your foolishness.

Eurota then asked:

"Why do thou blush, Telusa?"

Telusa answered:

"To hear thee in reckoning my pains to recite thine own.

"I saw, Eurota, how amorously you glanced your eye on the fair boy in the white coat, and how cunningly, now that you would have some talk of love, you metaphorically hit me in the teeth and reproach me with love."

Galatea wore a white coat as part of her disguise.

Eurota said:

"I confess that I am in love, and yet I swear that I don't know what it is. I feel my thoughts unknit and disjointed, my eyes unstayed [wandering] and unstaid [not sober], my heart I don't know how affected or infected, my sleeps broken and full of dreams, my waking hours sad and full of sighs, myself in all things unlike myself.

"If this is love, I wish that it had never been devised."

"Thou have told what I am in uttering what thyself is," Telusa said. "These are my passions, Eurota, my unbridled passions, my intolerable passions, which it would be as good for me to acknowledge and crave and seek counsel and advice as to deny and endure peril."

"How did it take you first, Telusa?" Eurota asked.

Telusa answered:

"By the eyes, my wanton eyes, which conceived the picture of his face and hanged it on the very strings of my heart.

"O fair Melebeus! O fond Telusa!"

Of course, Melebeus is the disguised Phillida.

Telusa then asked:

"But how did it take you, Eurota?"

Eurota answered:

"By the ears: Tityrus' sweet words have sunk so deep into my head that the remembrance of his wit and intelligence has bereaved me of my wisdom.

"O eloquent Tityrus!"

Of course, Tityrus is the disguised Galatea.

Eurota continued:

"O credulous Eurota!

"But quiet, here comes Ramia. But let her not hear us talk. We will withdraw a little distance away and hear her talk."

They concealed themselves.

Ramia entered the scene.

She said to herself, "I who have lost myself have been sent to seek others."

Eurota whispered to Telusa, "You shall see that Ramia has also bitten on a love-leaf and fallen in love."

Thinking herself to be alone, Ramia then said:

"Can there be no heart so chaste but love can wound it? Can there be no vows so holy but affection and love can violate them?

"Virtue, thou are vain, and thou, chastity, are just a byword and object of scorn, when you both are subject to love, of all things the most abject and debased.

"If Love is a god, why shouldn't lovers be virtuous? Love is a god, and lovers are virtuous."

Cupid is also known as Love.

Coming forward with Telusa, Eurota said, "Indeed, Ramia, if lovers were not virtuous, then thou would be vicious and given to vice."

"What!" Ramia said. "Have you come so near me?"

She was surprised that they had been so near her while she thought she was speaking to herself. Of course, she was worried that they had overheard her.

"I think we came near you when we said you loved," Telusa said.

"Come near me" means "understand me" as well as "come close to me."

Eurota said:

"Tush, Ramia, it is too late to recall it; to repent it would be a shame.

"Therefore, I ask thee to tell us what is love."

Ramia said:

"If only I myself felt this infection, I would then take upon me the definition, but, since this infection — love — is incident to so many, I dare not myself describe it.

"But we will all talk of that in the woods. Diana storms and rages that, sending one nymph to seek another, she loses all her nymphs.

"Servia, of all the nymphs the shyest and most reserved, loves excessively, and exclaims against Diana, honors Venus, detests Vesta, and makes a common scorn of virtue."

Vesta is the virgin goddess of the hearth.

Ramia continued:

"Clymene, whose stately looks seemed to amaze and confound the greatest lords, stoops, yields, and fawns on the strange boy in the woods. I myself (with blushing I speak it) am thrall to — that is, captivated by — that boy, that fair boy, that beautiful boy!"

Telusa said, "What have we here? All of us are in love? No other food than fancy? No, no, she shall not have the fair boy."

"Nor shall you, Telusa," Eurota said.

"Nor shall you, Eurota," Ramia said.

Each nymph believed that the other nymphs loved the boy she loved.

Telusa said, "I love Melebeus, and my deserts shall be answerable to my desires. I will forsake Diana for him. I will die for him!"

Of course, Melebeus is the disguised Phillida.

Ramia said:

"So says Clymene, and she says she will have him. I don't care.

"My sweet Tityrus, although he seems proud, I impute it to childishness, who, being yet scarcely out of swath-clouts — infant swaddling clothes — cannot understand these deep conceits and ideas. I love him."

"So do I, and I will have him!" Eurota said.

Telusa and Clymene loved the disguised Phillida, and Eurota and Ramia loved the disguised Galatea. Servia also loved someone.

Telusa said:

"Immodest that we all are, unfortunate that we all are likely to be, shall virgins begin to wrangle for love and become wanton in their thoughts, in their words, and in their actions?

"O divine Love, who are therefore called divine because thou overreach and overpower the wisest, conquer the chastest, and do all things both unlikely and impossible, because thou are Love!

"Thou make the bashful impudent, thou make the wise fond and foolish, thou make the chaste wanton and lascivious, and thou work contraries to our reach, because thou thyself are beyond reason."

Love does things that humans cannot understand because Love is beyond reason.

Love is not irrational, but it is non-rational.

Eurota said:

"Talk no more, Telusa; your words wound.

"Ah, I wish that I were not a woman!"

"I wish that Tityrus were not a boy!" Ramia said.

"I wish that Telusa were nobody!" Telusa said.

They exited.

Phillida and Galatea, both disguised as young men, talked together.

The disguised Phillida said, "It is a pity that Nature did not make you a woman, since you have so fair a face, so lovely a countenance, and so modest a behavior."

The disguised Galatea replied, "There is a tree in Tylos whose nuts have shells like fire, and being cracked, the kernel is just water."

These nuts are not what they seem to be, and neither is the disguised Galatea.

"What a toy — an idle fancy — is it to tell me of that tree, being nothing to the purpose?" Phillida said, not understanding. "I say it is a pity you are not a woman."

"I would not wish to be a woman unless it were because thou are a man," Galatea said.

"I do not wish to be a woman, for then I should not love thee, for I have sworn never to love a woman," Phillida said.

"That is a strange humor — whim — in so pretty a youth, and it is in accordance with mine, for I myself will never love a woman," Galatea said.

"It would be a shame if a maiden should be a suitor (a thing hated in that sex), and that then thou should decline to be her devoted servant, lover, and admirer," Phillida said.

"If it is a shame in me, it can be no commendation in you, for you yourself are of that mind — you have made the same decision that I have," Galatea said.

Phillida said:

"Suppose I were a virgin (I blush in supposing myself one), and that under the clothing of a boy were the person and body of a maiden.

"If I should utter my affection with sighs, manifest my sweet love by my salt tears, and prove my loyalty unspotted and my griefs intolerable, wouldn't then that fair face pity this true heart?"

Galatea said, "Admit [Suppose] that I were as you would have me suppose that you are, and that I should with entreaties, prayers, oaths, bribes, and whatever can be invented in love desire your favor. Would you then yield your love to me?"

"Bah, you come in with 'admit,'" Phillida said.

"And you come in with 'suppose,'" Galatea said.

Phillida said to herself, "What doubtful — ambiguous — speeches these are! I fear that he is as I am: a maiden."

Maidens are young female virgins.

Galatea said to herself, "What dread rises in my mind! I fear that the boy is as I am: a maiden."

Phillida said to herself, "Bah, it cannot be. His voice shows the contrary."

Galatea said to herself, "Yet I do not think it, for he would then have blushed."

"Have you any sisters?" Phillida asked.

"If I had only one sister, my brother must necessarily have two sisters," Galatea said. "But I ask, do you have a sister?"

"My father had only one daughter, and therefore I could have no sister," Phillida said.

Galatea said to herself, "Aye, me! Alas! He is as I am, for his speeches are as mine are."

Phillida said to herself, "What shall I do? Either he is subtle and cunning, or my female sex is simple and not astute."

Galatea said to herself, "I have known several of Diana's nymphs to be enamored of and in love with him, yet he has rejected all of them, either because he is too proud and disdains them, or because he is too childish and young to understand them, or because he knows himself to be a virgin."

Chances are excellent that she meant female virgin.

Phillida said to herself:

"I am in a quandary. Diana's nymphs have followed him, and he has rejected them, either knowing too well the beauty of his own face or that he himself is of the same shape and mold."

If the disguised Galatea were to be the same shape and mold as Diana's nymphs, she would have a female form.

Phillida said to herself:

"I will once again test him."

Phillida then said to the disguised Galatea:

"You promised me in the woods that you would love me before all of Diana's nymphs."

"Aye, as long as you would love me before all of Diana's nymphs," Galatea replied.

"Can you prefer a fond, foolish boy as I am before as fair ladies as they are?" Phillida asked.

"Why shouldn't I as well as you?" Galatea asked.

"Come, let us go into the grove, and make much of each other, who cannot tell what to think about each other," Phillida said.

They went into the grove.

Their speeches had made it clear that each of them was a young woman. If they seemed obtuse, it is because they did not want to accept the truth.

The alchemist and Rafe talked together.

"Rafe, my serving-boy has run away," the alchemist said. "I trust thou will not run after him."

Rafe said to himself, "I wish that I had a pair of wings so that I might fly after him!"

The alchemist continued, "My serving-boy was the veriest — the most thorough-going — thief, he was the most arrant — most downright — liar, and he was the vilest swearer in the world, but otherwise he was the best boy in the world. He has stolen my apparel and all my money, and he has forgotten nothing except to bid me farewell."

"That I will not forget," Rafe said. "Farewell, master!"

He turned to go.

"Why, thou have not yet seen the end of my art," the alchemist said.

By "end," the alchemist meant "outcome."

Rafe said:

"I wish that I had not known the beginning.

"Didn't you promise me that out of my silver thimble you would make a whole cupboard of silver-plated plates, and didn't you promise me that out of a Spanish needle you would build a silver steeple?"

The alchemist said:

"Aye, Rafe, I did promise those things.

"The fortune — the success — of this art consists in the precise measure of the fire, for if there is a coal too much or a spark too little, if the fire is a little too hot or a thought too soft and moderate, then all our labor is in vain.

"Besides, they who blow on the fire must beat time with their breaths, as musicians do with their breasts and breaths as they keep time while singing, because there must be a true harmony of the metals, the fire, and the workers."

Rafe said, "Nay, if you must weigh your fire by ounces, and take measure of a man's blast — that is, his breath — you may then make a wedge of gold from a dram of wind, and from the shadow of one shilling make another, as long as you have an organist to tune your temperatures."

"To weigh the fire and measure the wind" was proverbial for something impossible to do.

We can measure quantities of grain and appropriately mete them out to people, but no one can do that with wind.

An organist can play an organ, and in this context, an organist can control his breathing organs.

"So is it, and often does it happen, that the just proportion of the fire and all things concur," the alchemist said.

Rafe said:

"Con-cur? Con-dog!"

In other words: Concur? Don't con me! Con a dog!

Rafe then said:

"I will go away."

"Then go away!" the alchemist said.

The alchemist exited.

An astronomer entered the scene, gazing up at the sky, with an almanac in his hands. He and Rafe did not notice each other at first.

Rafe said about the astronomer:

"An art — so you say — that one multiplies so much all day that he lacks money to buy food at night?"

Seeing the astronomer, he said:

"But what have we yonder? What devout man?"

The astronomer was holding a book, many of which were devotional.

Rafe continued saying to himself:

"He will never speak until he is urged. I will greet him."

He then said out loud:

"Sir, there lies a purse under your feet. If I thought it were not yours, I would pick it up."

A purse is a container for money. In this society, men and woman had money containers that they called purses.

This astronomer was also an astrologer, and he would claim that nothing could happen that he did not know about ahead of time, but he had not foreknown that he would drop his purse and money.

The astronomer picked up his purse and asked, "Don't thou know that I was calculating the nativity — the horoscope — of Alexander's great horse?"

Ah, he had an excuse: He was busy with his astrological calculations or he would have stopped his purse from falling earlier.

Bucephalus was a beautiful horse, but no one could ride him. The young Alexander the Great noticed that Bucephalus was afraid of its own shadow. Alexander therefore had the horse face the sun as he trained it. Soon, Bucephalus lost its fear of its own shadow and became Alexander's war horse.

It's difficult to see why Alexander's great horse would need its nativity calculated. Horoscopes foretell the future. Bucephalus' future was to continue to be dead.

"Why, what are you?" Rafe asked.

"I am an astronomer."

"What! One of those who make almanacs?" Rafe asked.

Almanacs contained weather predictions and much astronomical and astrological data.

The astronomer said:

"*Ipsissimus.* The very one.

"I can tell the minute of thy birth, the moment of thy death, and the manner how thee will die. I can tell thee what weather shall be between this moment and *octogessimus octavus mirabilis annus.*"

The *mirabilis annus* — the miracle year — was '88, aka 1588. Astrologers forecast disasters and catastrophes for that year, but 1588 was the year the English navy defeated the Spanish Armada.

The astronomer continued:

"When I want to, I can set a trap for the sun, catch the moon with lime-twigs, and go a-batfowling for stars."

Twigs smeared with sticky lime were used to catch birds.

In batfowling, bats were dazzled with light and caught at night.

The astronomer continued:

"I can tell thee things past and things to come, and with my cunning measure I can tell thee how many yards of clouds are beneath the sky."

How many yards of clouds are beneath the sky? None. Clouds are in the sky.

The astronomer continued:

"Nothing can happen that I do not foresee; nothing shall."

"I hope, sir, you are no more than a god," Rafe said.

"I can bring the twelve signs out of their zodiacs and hang them up at taverns," the astronomer said.

Many taverns were named after signs of the zodiac and celestial bodies.

"I ask you, sir, to tell me what you cannot do," Rafe said, "for I perceive there is nothing as easy for you to encompass as impossibilities. But what are those signs?"

The astronomer said:

"As a man should say, signs that govern the body."

According to astrologers, each zodiac sign governed — affected — a part of the human body.

The astronomer continued:

"The ram governs the head."

"That is the worst sign for the head," Rafe said.

"Why?" the astronomer asked.

"Because it is a sign of an ill ewe," Rafe said.

On their heads, rams have horns, which is the sign of a cuckold: a man with an unfaithful wife. Here, the unfaithful wife is an ill ewe.

An ill ewe can make you an ill you if you are married to one.

"Bah, that sign must be there," the astronomer said. "Then the Bull for the throat, Capricornus for the knees."

Rafe said:

"I will hear no more signs if they are all such desperate and discouraging signs.

"But seeing you are — I don't know what to call you — shall I serve you? I would like to serve you."

"I accept thee," the astronomer said.

Rafe said, "I am happy! For now I shall reach lofty thoughts, and count how many drops of water go into the greatest shower of rain. You shall see me catch the moon in the 'clips like a coney in a purse-net."

The 'clips is 1) an eclipse, and 2) pincers or forceps.

A coney is a rabbit, and a purse-net is a net with a drawstring opening. The net was used to trap rabbits.

"I will teach thee the golden number, the epact, and the prime," the astronomer said.

Rafe did not know these astronomical terms, and you, the readers, don't need to know them, unless you have a need to learn astronomical jargon.

Rafe said:

"I will meddle no more with the numbering — the measuring — of gold, for multiplication is a miserable action.

"Please tell me, sir, what weather shall we have this hour in threescore years — in sixty years?"

The astronomer said:

"That I must cast by our judicials astronomical."

Judicials astronomical are a system for making astrological predictions based on the positions and influences of heavenly bodies.

The astronomer continued:

"Therefore, come in with me, and thou shall see every wrinkle in my astrological wisdom, and I will make the heavens as plain to thee as the highway.

A wrinkle is 1) an adroit — clever — action, or 2) a crafty trick.

The astronomer continued:

"Thy cunning shall sit cheek by jowl with the sun's chariot.

"Then shall thou see what a base thing it is to have others' thoughts creep on the ground, when thine shall be stitched to the stars."

Rafe said, "Then I shall be translated from this mortality."

If Rafe were to ride in the sun-chariot beside Helios or Apollo, he would be unlikely to be mortal.

The human condition is that we are mortal, and we will die.

"Thy thoughts shall be metamorphosed and made hail-fellows — good friends — with the gods," the astronomer said.

Rafe said:

"O Lady Fortune!

"I feel my very brains moralized, and as it were, a certain contempt of earthly actions has crept into my mind by an ethereal and sublime contemplation.

"Come, let us go in."

According to the *Oxford English Dictionary*, one definition of "moralize" is "To interpret morally or symbolically; to explain the moral meaning of (an event, etc.)." Another meaning is "To make moral."

Apparently, Rafe is saying that his brains have become moral, and he can look at earthly actions and find them contemptible.

If he finds all earthly actions contemptible, his education is incomplete, as human beings are capable of much good as well as of much evil.

They exited.

The goddess Diana and the nymphs Telusa, Eurota, Ramia, and Larissa talked together.

Diana said:

"What news have we here, ladies? Are all my nymphs in love? Have Diana's nymphs become Venus' wanton women? Is it a shame to be chaste because you are amiable? Or must you necessarily be amorous because you are fair and beautiful?"

A proverb stated, "Beauty and chastity (honesty) seldom meet."

Diana continued:

"O Venus, if this is thy spite, I will requite it with more than hate. Well shall thou know what it is to drib — to shoot poorly — thine arrows up and down Diana's leas — Diana's meadows."

The arrows belonged to Venus' son: Cupid.

Diana continued:

"There is an unknown nymph who wanders up and down these woods, who I suspect has been the weaver of these woes. I saw her slumbering by the brook-side. Go search for her and bring her here.

"If you find upon her shoulder a burn, it is Cupid; if you find any print on her back like a leaf, it is Medea; if you find any picture on her left breast like a bird, it is Calypso."

Venus was jealous of the mortal woman Psyche, and she sent Cupid to kill her, but Cupid fell in love with the mortal Psyche, and he made a home for her and slept with her on the condition that she never see his face. Curious, Psyche looked at his face by candlelight as he was sleeping, and some candlewax fell on him and burned him. He fled, and Psyche wandered the earth in search of him. After many trials, Psyche became immortal, and she and her husband, Cupid, had a daughter named Pleasure.

The story of Psyche and Cupid is told in *The Golden Ass* by Apuleius.

Medea was a witch who had much knowledge of medicinal herbs and of poisonous herbs. She helped Jason of the Argonauts fame to get the golden fleece.

The story of Medea and Jason is told in Apollonius of Rhodes' *Argonautica* and in Euripides' tragedy *Medea*.

Calypso was a goddess who kept Ulysses prisoner for seven years before allowing him to return to his home island of Ithaca.

The story of Calypso and Odysseus, aka Ulysses, is told in Homer's *Odyssey*.

Diana continued:

"Whoever it is, bring her here, and speedily bring her here."

"I will go with speed," Telusa said.

"Go, Larissa, and help her," Diana said.

"I obey," Larissa said.

Telusa and Larissa exited.

Diana said:

"Now, ladies, doesn't what makes my ears glow make your cheeks blush?"

A proverb stated, "When your ear tingles (burns), people are talking about you."

Diana continued:

"Or can you remember without sobs that which Diana cannot think about without sighs?

"What greater dishonor could happen to Diana, or to her nymphs' shame, than that there can be any time so idle that should make their heads so addled and confused?"

This society believed that leisure was conducive to falling in love.

Diana continued:

"Your chaste hearts, my nymphs, should resemble the onyx, which is hottest when it is whitest; and your thoughts, the more they are assaulted with desires, the less they should be affected. You should think that love is like Homer's moly: a white leaf and a black root, a fair show and a bitter taste."

In the *Odyssey*, Hermes gave Odysseus (his Roman name is Ulysses) the plant moly, which protected him against the goddess Circe, who attempted to transform him into a pig.

A proverb stated, "Beauty may have fair leaves yet bitter fruit."

Diana continued:

"Of all trees the cedar is greatest and has the smallest seed; of all affections, love has the greatest name — the greatest reputation — and the least virtue."

A proverb stated, "Of [From] little seeds grow great cedars (trees)."

Diana continued:

"Shall it be said, and shall Venus say it — nay, shall it be seen, and shall wantons see it — that Diana, the goddess of chastity, whose thoughts are always answerable to her vows, whose eyes never glanced on desire, and whose heart abates and blunts the point of Cupid's arrows, shall have her virgins become unchaste in desires, immoderate in affection, and intemperate in love ... in foolish love ... in base love?"

"Eagles cast their evil feathers in the sun, but you cast your best desires upon a shadow."

Some people in this society had heard the folk belief that old eagles fly high into the air so the sun would heat them and open their pores so the eagles could shed their feathers. The eagles dived into water, which renewed their feathers and made the eagles young again.

Diana continued:

"The Egyptian birds known as *ibes* lose their sweetness when they lose their sights, and virgins lose all their virtues with their unchaste thoughts.

"Diana calls 'unchaste' that which has either any show or any suspicion of lightness: unchastity."

Women with light heels have legs that can easily be raised into the air for the missionary position.

Diana continued:

"O my dear nymphs, if you knew how loving thoughts stain lovely faces, you would be as careful to have your thoughts as unspotted as your face is beautiful.

"Cast before your eyes the loves of Venus' trulls — promiscuous women — their fortunes, their fancies, their ends and fates. What else are they but Silenus' pictures — outside, good things such as lambs and doves; inside, bad things such as apes and owls. These trulls, like Ixion, embrace clouds for Juno; they embrace the shadows of virtue instead of the substance of virtue."

In ancient Greece, images of Silenus, the drunk and jovial companion of Bacchus, could be opened to reveal an image of gods. Silenus is often regarded as ugly, but his personality may be greatly preferred to those of the Olympian gods, many or all of whom were often petty, vindictive, and entirely capable of rape. Neptune, of course, required the sacrifice of a virgin every five years.

Better a drunk, jovial god than a petty, bloodthirsty god.

Ixion, the King of the Lapiths, who violated proper guest-host relations, was bound to a continually spinning fiery wheel in the Land of the Dead. Among his sins was attempting to rape Juno while he was one of Jupiter's guests. To prevent the rape, Jupiter made a cloud in the shape of Juno. Ixion coupled with it, and from this union came Imbros, aka Centaurus, who mated with mares and created the Centaurs, most of whom were wild.

A proverb stated, "Lose not the substance for the shadow."

Diana continued:

"The eagle's feathers consume the feathers of all others, and love's desire corrupts all other virtues."

Some people in this society believed that if an eagle's feathers were placed near other feathers, the eagle's feathers would destroy the other feathers.

Diana continued:

"I blush, ladies, that you, having been heretofore patient and enduring of labors, should now become apprentices to idleness and use the pen for sonnets, not the needle for samplers.

"And how and where is your love placed? Upon pelting, paltry boys, perhaps base of birth, without doubt weak of discretion.

"'Aye, but they are fair.'

"O ladies, do your eyes begin to love colors — to love appearances, which may be false — whose hearts were accustomed to loathe them? Has Diana's chase — Diana's hunting ground — become Venus' court? And are your holy vows turned to hollow thoughts?"

Ramia said, "Madam, if love were not a thing beyond reason, we might then give a reason for our doings; but so divine is his force that it works effects as contrary to that we wish as unreasonable against that we ought."

"Lady, we are so unacquainted and unfamiliar with the passions of love that we can neither describe them nor bear them," Eurota said.

Diana said:

"Foolish girls, how willing you are to follow that which you should flee!

"But here comes Telusa."

Telusa and Larissa returned with Cupid.

Telusa said, "We have brought the disguised nymph, and we have found on his shoulder Psyche's burn, and he confesses that he is Cupid."

Diana said to Cupid, "How are you now, sir? Are you caught? Are you Cupid?"

Cupid replied, "Thou shall see, Diana, that I dare confess myself to be Cupid."

Diana said:

"And thou shall see, Cupid, that I will show myself to be Diana — that is, I am the conqueror of thy loose and untamed appetites. Did thy mother, Venus, under the color — the disguise — of a nymph, send thee hither to wound my nymphs? Does she add craft to her malice, and, mistrusting her deity, practice deceit? Is there no place but my groves? Are there no persons but my nymphs?

"Cruel and unkind Venus, who spites only chastity, thou shall see that Diana's power shall revenge thy policy — thy trickery and thy scheming — and tame this pride.

"As for thee, Cupid, I will break thy bow and burn thine arrows, bind thy hands, clip thy wings, and fetter thy feet. Thou who fatten and feed others with hopes shall be fed with wishes, and thou who bind others with golden thoughts shall be bound with golden fetters. Venus' rods are made of roses; Diana's rods are made of briars."

Rods are canes.

Venus and Cupid sometimes wore chaplets made of roses.

Hawthorn is associated with the nightingale and with Diana: with true love and with chastity.

Diana continued:

"Let Venus, that great goddess, ransom Cupid, that little god.

"These ladies here, whom thou — Cupid — have infected with foolish love, shall both tread on thee and triumph over thee. Thine own arrow shall be shot into thine own bosom, and thou shall be enamored, not on Psyches, but on Circes."

Psyche was beautiful, loving, and mortal but became immortal.

The goddess Circe transformed Ulysses' men into pigs.

Diana continued:

"I will teach thee what it is to displease Diana, distress her nymphs, and disturb her game."

Her "game" is her entertainment, and it is the animals she hunts.

Cupid said, "Diana, what I have done cannot be undone, but what you mean to do shall be undone. Venus has some gods who are her friends, and Cupid shall have all."

In other words: Cupid shall have the victory, and he shall have all the other gods on his side.

Diana replied:

"Are you prating and chattering without purpose? I will bridle and curb thy tongue and thy power, and in spite of my own thoughts I will set thee a task every day which, if thou do not finish it, thou shall feel the smart. Thou shall be treated as Diana's slave, not Venus' son. All the world shall see that I will treat thee like a captive, and I will show that I am a conqueror."

She then said to her nymphs:

"Come, bring him in, so that we may devise apt punishments for his proud presumptions."

Eurota said to Cupid, "We will plague you as a little god."

Telusa said to Cupid, "We will never pity thee, although thou are a god."

Ramia said to Cupid, "Nor will I pity thee."

Larissa said to Cupid, "Nor will I pity thee."

They exited.

CHAPTER 4
— 4.1 —

An augur, Melebeus, Tityrus, and two countrymen met together.

Augurs foretell the future, and they prepare sacrifices.

The augur said:

"This is the day on which you must satisfy Neptune and save yourselves. Call together your fair daughters, and for a sacrifice take the most beautiful, for it is better to offer a virgin than to suffer ruin."

A proverb stated, "Better one die (perish, suffer) than all."

The sacrifice was a bribe to the god Neptune: Take this one life and protect the lives of the rest of us.

So said the augur.

Asshole.

If a god is not good, then that god ought not to be worshipped. The word "worshipped" means "adored."

Why give such a god a priest? Or an augur? Or a sacrifice?

The augur continued:

"If you think it against natural affection and love to sacrifice your children, think it also against sense to destroy your country. If you imagine Neptune pitiless to desire such a prey, confess yourselves perverse to deserve such a punishment.

"You see this tree, this fatal tree, whose leaves, although they glitter like gold, yet the tree threatens grief to beautiful virgins.

"To this tree the most beautiful virgin must be bound until the monster Agar carries her away, and, if the monster does not come, then assure yourselves that the most beautiful virgin is concealed; and then your country shall be destroyed.

"Therefore, consult with yourselves, not as fathers of children, but as favorers of your country. Let Neptune have his right — have what is due to him — if you wish to have your quiet.

"Thus I have warned you to be careful, and I would wish you to be wise, knowing that who has the fairest daughter has the greatest fortune, in losing one to save all. And so I depart to provide ceremonies for the sacrifice, and I command you to bring the sacrifice."

The augur exited.

Both Melebeus and Tityrus had beautiful daughters they had disguised and hidden. Neither wanted his own daughter to be a sacrifice to Neptune. If someone's daughter had to die, each father preferred that she be the other father's daughter.

Melebeus said, "They say, Tityrus, that you have a beautiful daughter. If it is true, then don't lie, for you shall be a fortunate father because it is a thing holy to preserve one's country, and it is honorable to be the cause."

Tityrus replied, "Indeed, Melebeus, I have heard you boast that you had a fair daughter than whom no one was more beautiful. I hope you are not so full of care for a child that you will be lacking regard for your country, and I hope you will not add so much to natural affection and love that you will detract from wisdom and impair your reasoning."

Melebeus said:

"I must confess that I had a daughter, and I know that you have a daughter — but alas! My child's cradle was her grave, and her swath-clout — her swaddling cloth that she was wrapped in when she was born — was her winding sheet, aka shroud.

"I wish that she had lived until now. She would willingly have died now; for what could have happened to poor Melebeus more comfortable and satisfying than to be the father of a fair child and sweet country?"

Tityrus said:

"Oh, Melebeus, you may dissemble with men, but you cannot deceive the gods. Didn't I see (and very recently see) your daughter in your arms, when you gave her infinite kisses with affection that I fear were more than fatherly?

"You have conveyed and stolen her away so that you might cast us all away and destroy us, bereaving and depriving her of the honor of her beauty and bereaving us of the benefit, preferring a common harm before a private evil."

A proverb states, "Private welfare is not to be preferred before common-weal."

Melebeus said:

"It is a bad cloth, Tityrus, that will take no dye-color, and it is a simple, foolish father who can use no cunning. You make the people believe that you wish well when you practice and engage in nothing but ill, wishing to be thought religious towards the gods when I know you are deceitful towards men.

"You cannot overreach and outwit me, Tityrus, but you may overshoot yourself and what you are capable of. It is a wily mouse that will breed in the cat's ear, and he must halt — limp — cunningly who will deceive a cripple.

"Did you ever see me kiss my daughter? You are deceived; it was my wife whom I kissed. And if you thought so young a piece — that is, a woman — unfit for so old a person, and therefore imagined it to be my child, not my spouse, you must know that silver hairs delight in golden locks, and the old fancies and appetites crave young nurses, and frosty years must be thawed by youthful fires.

"But this matter set aside, you have a fair daughter, Tityrus, and it is a pity you are so fond and doting a father."

One of the countrymen said, "You are both either too fond and foolish or too froward and disobedient, for, while you dispute to save your daughters, we neglect to prevent our destruction."

The other countryman said, "Come, let us go away and seek out a sacrifice. We must sift and examine these two fathers' cunning, and we must let them shift for and look after themselves."

They exited.

Telusa, Eurota, and Larissa sang a song. Cupid and Ramia listened.

Telusa sang:

"Oyez! Oyez!"

"Oyez" means "Be quiet and pay attention."

Telusa continued to sing:

"If any maid [maiden]

"Whom leering Cupid has betrayed

"To frowns of spite [vexation], to eyes of scorn,

"And would in madness now see torn

"The boy in pieces —"

Telusa, Eurota, and Larissa sang:

"Let her come

"Hither and lay on him her doom [verdict]."

Eurota sang:

"Oyez! Oyez!

"Has any lost

"A heart which many a sigh has cost?"

A folk belief alleged that one sigh resulted in the loss of one drop of blood from the heart.

Eurota continued to sing:

"Is any cozened [cheated] of a tear,

"Which, as a pearl, Disdain does wear?

"Here stands the thief."

Telusa, Eurota, and Larissa sang:

"Let her but come

"Hither, and lay on him her doom [verdict]."

Larissa sang:

"Is any one undone [ruined] by fire,"

"Fire" is the fire of love.

Larissa continued to sing:

"And turned to ashes through desire?
"Did ever any lady weep,
"Being cheated of her golden sleep?
"Stol'n by sick thoughts?"
Telusa, Eurota, and Larissa sang:
"The pirate's found,
"And in her tears he shall be drowned.
"Read his indictment; let him hear
"What he's to trust to [look for]."
She then said to Cupid:
"Boy, give ear! Listen!"
Telusa said, "Come, Cupid, get to work on your task. First you must undo all these lovers' knots because you tied them."

Cupid said, "If they are true love-knots, it is impossible to unknit — to untie — them; if they are false love-knots, I never tied them."

"Make no excuse, but go to it," Eurota said. "Get to work."

Cupid said:

"Love-knots are tied with eyes and cannot be undone with hands; love-knots are made tight with thoughts and cannot be unloosed with fingers. Doesn't Diana have any task to set Cupid to work on other than impossible tasks?"

The nymphs threatened him.

Cupid then said:

"I will get to work on it."

He set to work, unwillingly, on a love-knot.

"Why, what is this now?" Ramia said. "You tie the knots tighter."

"I cannot choose to do otherwise," Cupid said. "It goes against my mind and my nature to make them loose."

Eurota said:

"Let me see, now."

She tried to untie the love-knot, and then she said:

"It is impossible to be undone."

Cupid explained, "It is the true love-knot of a woman's heart, and therefore it cannot be undone."

He tried to untie another love-knot and easily untied it.

"That falls in sunder of itself," Ramia said. "That love-knot falls apart by itself."

"It was made from a man's thought, which will never hang together and remain consistent," Cupid explained.

"You have untied that well," Larissa said.

"Aye, because it was never tied well," Cupid said.

Telusa said:

"Get to work on the rest, for Diana will give you no rest."

Cupid resumed his task and untied two love-knots.

Telusa then said:

"These two knots are finely and easily untied!"

Cupid explained, "It was because I never tied them. The one love-knot was knit by Pluto, not Cupid, by money, not love; the other love-knot was knit by force, not faith, by appointment and orders, not affection."

Pluto is the god of the Land of the Dead, aka the Underworld. Much wealth, such as diamonds and gold, comes from underground.

Some matches are made by parents, not by the man and the woman. Some marriages are arranged.

Cupid tried to untie another love-knot but gave up.

"Why do you lay that knot aside?" Ramia asked.

"I lay it aside for Death," Cupid said.

"Why?" Telusa asked.

"Because the knot was knit by faith, and it must only be unknit by Death," Cupid said.

He picked up another love-knot, and then he laughed.

"Why do you laugh?" Eurota asked.

"Because it is both the most beautiful and the most false, done with the greatest art and the least truth, with the best colors and the worst conceits — the finest shows and the worst designs," Cupid explained.

"Who tied it?" Telusa asked.

"A man's tongue." Cupid answered.

He bestowed the love-knot on Larissa.

"Why do you put that in my bosom?" Larissa asked.

"Because it is only for a woman's bosom," Cupid answered.

"Why, what is it?" Larissa asked.

"A woman's heart," Cupid answered.

Telusa said to Ramia and Eurota:

"Come, let us go in and tell Diana that Cupid has done his task."

She then said:

"You stay behind, Larissa, and see to it that Cupid does not sleep, for love will be idle. And take heed you don't surfeit and overindulge in Cupid's company, for love will be wanton."

"Let me alone and leave it to me," Larissa said. "I will find him something to do."

Telusa exited with Ramia and Eurota.

"Lady, can you for pity see Cupid thus punished?" Cupid asked.

"Why did Cupid punish us without pity?" Larissa asked.

He had punished the nymphs by making them fall in love.

"Is love a punishment?" Cupid asked.

"It is no pastime, no game, no pleasurable entertainment," Larissa answered.

Cupid said to the absent Venus:

"O Venus, if thou saw Cupid as a captive, bound to obey who was accustomed to command, fearing ladies' threats who once pierced their hearts, I cannot tell whether thou would revenge it for despite or laugh at it for disport."

"For despite" means "out of anger and indignation and offended pride," and "for disport" means "for amusement."

Cupid said to the absent Diana:

"The time may come, Diana, and the time shall come, that thou who set Cupid to undo love-knots shall entreat Cupid to tie love-knots."

Cupid said to the women reading this book:

"And you ladies who with solace and pleasure have beheld my pains shall with sighs entreat my pity."

Cupid then started to go to sleep.

"What is this now, Cupid?" Larissa asked. "Do you begin to nod with sleepiness?"

Ramia, Telusa, and Eurota entered the scene.

Ramia said:

"Come, Cupid, Diana has devised new labors for you who are the god of loves. You shall weave samplers all night, and lackey after — be a servant to — Diana all day. You shall shortly shoot at beasts instead of men because you have made beasts of men by making their passion for love overcome their reason, and you shall wait on ladies' trains [retinues] because thou entrap ladies by trains [tricks].

"All the stories that are in Diana's arras — her wall hanging decorated with woven pictures — which are about love you must pick out — must unpick — with your needle, and in that place sew Vesta with her nuns and Diana with her nymphs.

"How do you like this, Cupid?"

"I say that I will prick as well with my needle as ever I did with my arrows," Cupid said.

Hmm. In the slang of this society, a "needle' is a penis.

"Diana cannot yield," Telusa said. "She conquers affection and love."

These are famous last words.

"Diana shall yield," Cupid said. "She cannot conquer destiny."

"Come, Cupid, you must go to your business and task," Larissa said.

"You shall find me so busy in your heads — so active in your thoughts — that you shall wish that I had been idle with your hearts," Cupid said.

Cupid and Larissa exited.

Alone, Neptune said to himself:

"This day is the solemn sacrifice at this tree; this is the day on which the fairest and most beautiful virgin (if the inhabitants weren't faithless and lacking in piety) should be offered to me. But so over-full of care are fathers for their children that they forget the safety of their country, and fearing to become unnatural and not show love for their children, they become unreasonable.

"Their sleights and tricks may blear and blur and deceive the eyes of men; they cannot deceive me. I will be here at the hour appointed for the sacrifice, and I will show as great cruelty as they have done crafty tricks, and they shall know well that Neptune should have been entreated, not cozened and cheated."

He exited.

The disguised Galatea and the disguised Phillida talked together. Still, neither knew that the other was a young woman although each suspected that the other was a young woman.

Phillida said, "I wonder which virgin the people will present for the sacrifice. It is fortunate you are not a female virgin, for then it would have fallen to your lot because you are so beautiful."

"If you had been a maiden, too, I need not to have feared because you are more beautiful than I am," Galatea said.

"Please, sweet boy, don't flatter me," Phillida said. "Speak the truth about thyself, for in my eye of all the world thou are the most beautiful."

"These are fair words, but far from thy true thoughts," Galatea said. "I know my own face in a true mirror, and I do not desire to see it in a flattering mouth."

Phillida said:

"Oh, I wish that I did flatter thee, and I wish that fortune would not flatter me!"

The first "flatter" means "overpraise," and the second "flatter" means "fill me with false hopes."

Phillida wished that she did overpraise Galatea's beauty, for if she did, Galatea would not become a sacrifice.

Phillida continued:

"I love thee as a brother, but thou do not love me in that way."

"No, I will not love thee as a brother, but I will love thee better because I cannot love as a brother," Galatea said.

"We are both boys, and we are both lovers," Phillida said. "So that our affection may have some expression and so that our affection for each other may seem as if it were love, let me call thee 'mistress.'"

"I accept that name, for several people before this time have called me mistress," Galatea said.

"For what reason?" Phillida asked.

Galatea replied, "Nay, there lie the mistress-ies: the mysteries."

"Will thou be at the sacrifice?" Phillida asked.

"No," Galatea said.

"Why?" Phillida asked

Galatea said:

"Because I dreamt that if I were there I would be turned into a virgin, and then being so beautiful (as thou say I am) I should be offered as a sacrifice, as thou know one must.

"But will you be there?"

"Not unless I were sure that a boy would be sacrificed, and not a maiden," Phillida said.

"Why, then you would be in danger," Galatea said.

"But I would escape it by deceit," Phillida said. "But seeing we are resolved to be both absent, let us wander into these groves until the hour of the sacrifice has passed."

"I am agreed, for then my fear will be past," Galatea said.

"Why, what do thou fear?" Phillida asked.

"Nothing except that you do not love me," Galatea said.

She exited.

Phillida said:

"I will love you."

She then said to herself:

"Poor Phillida, what should thou think of thyself, who love one who, I am afraid, is as thyself is: a female virgin?

"And can't it be possible that her father practiced the same deceit with her that my father has with me, and, knowing her to be fair, feared she should be unfortunate?

"If it is so, Phillida, how desperate and hopeless is thy case! If it is not so, how doubtful and uncertain! For if she is a maiden, there is no hope of my love; and if she is a boy, she is a hazard — there is only a chance and not a certainty for me to have her."

Hazards is a game played with two dice; a player can either win or lose it. In real tennis, hazards are openings into which the ball can be hit; hazards are especially those openings that do not win a point.

Phillida concluded:

"I will go after him or her, and I will lead a melancholy life, I who expect a miserable death."

She exited.

CHAPTER 5
— 5.1 —

Alone, Rafe said to himself:

"No more masters now, but a mistress, if I can alight on her."

A "mistress" is a female boss, or a female lover. He wanted to 1) find a female boss, and 2) climb on a female lover.

Rafe continued:

"An astronomer! Of all occupations that's the worst. Yet I hope that the alchemist may fare well, for he keeps good fires although he gets no gold.

"The other — the astronomer — stands warming himself by staring on the stars, which I think he can as soon and as easily count as know their properties. He told me a long tale about *octogessimus octavus*, the year 1588, and the meeting of the conjunctions and planets, and in the meantime he fell backward into a pond. I asked him why he had not foreseen that by the stars. He said he knew about it, but he disdained it and regarded it with contempt.

"But wait, isn't this my brother Robin?"

Entering the scene, Robin overheard him and said, "Yes, as sure as thou are Rafe."

"What! Robin?" Rafe said. "What is your news? What has been your luck and your fortune?"

Robin answered, "Indeed, I have had only bad fortune, but I ask thee to tell me thine fortune."

Rafe said:

"I have had two masters, not by art but by nature."

He did not find his two masters through his own efforts but came across them accidentally.

Also, the alchemist and the astronomer were unlikely to be masters by virtue of having university degrees; they were masters only because Rafe was their servant.

Rafe continued:

"One said that by multiplying he would make of a penny ten pounds."

"Aye, but could he do it?" Robin asked.

"Could he do it, you ask?" Rafe said. "Why, man, I saw a pretty wench come into his shop, where with puffing, blowing, and sweating, he so plied her that he multiplied her."

"Plied her." Nudge, nudge. Wink, wink.

"How?" Robin asked.

"Why he made her from one, two," Rafe said.

In other words: He made her pregnant.

"What, by fire?" Robin asked.

"No, by the philosopher's stone," Rafe said.

The philosopher's stone was supposed to be able to turn base metals such as iron into valuable metals such as gold.

"Why, do philosophers have such stones?" Robin asked.

In Elizabethan slang, "stones" are testicles.

"Aye, but they lie in a privy cupboard," Rafe said.

Anatomists call that private cupboard a scrotum.

"Why, then thou are rich if thou have learned this cunning knowledge," Robin said.

"Tush, this was nothing," Rafe said. "He would from a little fasting spittle make a hose and doublet of cloth of silver."

"Fasting spittle" is saliva that is generated from the smell of food when one has not eaten for a long time

Because of hunger, the alchemist would drool strands of saliva on his clothing.

Cloth of silver has silver threads woven into it.

Robin said, "I wish that I had been with him! For I have had almost no food but spittle since I came to the woods."

He swallowed a lot of saliva. The food he had had was mostly "food."

Also, the "spittle" may be charity and free food provided by 'spital — kind and hospitable — people.

Charitable people can be found in the countryside.

"How then did thou live?" Rafe asked.

"Why, man, I served a fortune-teller, who said I should live to see my father hanged and both my brothers beg," Robin said. "So I conclude the mill shall be mine, and I live by imagination still."

He stayed alive by constantly thinking about his future prospect of owning the family mill.

Rafe said:

"Thy master was an ass and looked on the lines of thy hands — he was a palm reader.

"But my other master was an astronomer, who could pick my nativity — my horoscope — out of the stars. I should have half a dozen stars in my pocket if I have not lost them, but here they are: Sol, Saturn, Jupiter, Mars, Venus."

Sol is the Sun. Saturn, Jupiter, Mars, and Venus are wandering stars, aka planets. They change positions in the night sky, while the fixed stars of the constellations do not change positions in relation to each other.

Rafe showed Robin a list of astrological names.

"Why, these are only names," Robin said.

"Aye, but by these he gathers that I was a Jovalist born of a Thursday, and that I should be a splendid Venerian and get all my good luck on a Friday," Rafe said.

A Jovalist is someone born on a day ruled by Jove, aka Jupiter: Thursday.

Rafe is lecherous, and he is lucky on Friday, the day ruled by Venus, and so he is also a Venerian.

"It is strange that a fish day should be a flesh-day," Robin said.

Fish days are days when many Christians eat fish rather than flesh. Venus' flesh day is devoted to a different kind of flesh than meat, and it is devoted to a different kind of activity than fasting.

Rafe spoke some Latin to his brother and translated it:

"Robin, *Venus orta mari*: Venus was born from the sea."

He continued:

"The sea will have fish, fish must have wine, wine will have flesh, for *caro carnis genus est muliebre*."

Wine increases sexual desire.

The Latin means, "*Caro, carnis* is feminine."

Many languages have masculine, feminine, and neuter cases.

Caro, carnis are Latin words for "flesh."

Rafe then said:

"But quiet, here comes that notable villain who once recommended me to the alchemist."

Peter entered the scene, not seeing the other two at first.

He said to himself, "As long as I had a master, I would not care what became of me."

Rafe whispered:

"Robin, thou shall see me fit him — that is, treat him appropriately.

"As long as I had a servant, I don't care about his moral and social conditions, his qualities and abilities, or his person, aka body."

Seeing them, Peter said, "What, Rafe? We are well met. No doubt you had a warm service from my master the alchemist?"

Rafe said:

"It was warm indeed, for the fire had almost burned out my eyes, and yet my teeth still watered with hunger, so that my service was both too hot and too cold. I melted all my meat — perspired and lost weight — and ate only my slumber thoughts, aka dreams, and so I had a full head and an empty belly."

It was a warm service of work, but not a warm service of food.

Rafe then asked:

"But where have thou been since?"

"With a brother of thine, I think, for he has such a coat as yours, and two brothers (as he said) seeking their fortunes," Peter said.

"It is my brother Dick," Robin said. "Please, let's go to him."

"Sirrah, what was he doing that he did not come with thee?" Rafe asked Peter.

"He has gotten a master now, who will teach him to make you both his younger brothers," Peter said.

It sounded as if the new master is a lawyer or a Sophist, or both.

In ancient Greece, Sophists were accused of teaching students how to make the weaker argument seem better than the stronger argument. They learned how to argue for both sides of a controversy: for and against.

"Aye, thou excel when it comes to devising impossibilities," Rafe said. "That's as true as thy master could make silver pots of tags of points."

"Nay, his master will teach him to cozen — cheat — you both, and so get the mill to himself," Peter said.

Rafe said:

"Nay, if he is both our cozens — our cousins and our cheats — I will be his great-grandfather, and Robin shall be his uncle."

This age was one of primogeniture. The eldest son would inherit most or all of the father's property and possessions.

In Elizabethan times, the word "cousin" had a wider meaning than it has today: It meant "kinsman."

Based on what Rafe had said, Rafe was the eldest son, and Dick was the youngest of the three sons.

Rafe believed that he and Robin could outcheat Dick, if necessary.

Rafe then said:

"But I ask thee to bring us to him quickly, for I am great-bellied with conceit — with curiosity — until I see him."

"Come then and go with me, and I will bring you to him straightaway," Peter said.

They exited.

The augur and Ericthinis, who was a countryman, talked together. Ericthinis' daughter, Hebe, had been chosen to be the sacrifice. She was not a volunteer.

The augur said, "Bring forth the virgin, the fatal — condemned by fate — virgin, the fairest and most beautiful virgin, if you mean to appease Neptune and preserve your country."

Ericthinis said, "Here she comes, accompanied only by men, because it is a sight unseemly (as all virgins say) to see the misfortune of a maiden, and it is terrible to behold the fierceness of Agar the monster."

Hebe, with some men, entered the scene where the sacrifice to Neptune would be held.

The men bound her to the tree.

Hebe lamented her fate:

"Miserable and accursed is Hebe, because although thou are neither fair and beautiful nor fortunate and happy, thou have been thought to be most happy and most beautiful!"

People have thought her to be most happy because as a sacrifice she could save her people from the wrath of Neptune.

People have thought her to be most beautiful because she was the most beautiful virgin they could find.

Hebe continued:

"Curse thy birth, thy life, thy death, being born to live in danger, and having lived, to die by deceit."

Because she was not beautiful, Hebe ought not to be the sacrifice. She was the sacrifice only because of the deceit of the fathers of Galatea and Phillida. These fathers had made their daughters dress in men's clothing so that they would not be chosen to be the sacrifice to Neptune.

Hebe continued:

"Are thou the sacrifice to appease Neptune and satisfy the custom, the bloody custom, ordained for the safety of thy country? Aye, Hebe, poor Hebe: men will have it so, whose strong forces command our weak natures. Indeed, the gods will have it so, whose powers make sport of and play with our purposes and plans.

"The Egyptians never cut their dates from the tree, because they were so fresh and green; it is thought wickedness to pull roses from the stalks in the garden of Palestine, because they have so lively a red; and anyone who cuts the incense tree in Arabia before it falls commits sacrilege.

"Shall it uniquely be lawful among us in the prime of youth and pride of beauty to destroy both youth and beauty? And what was honored in fruits and flowers as a virtue shall it uniquely be lawful among us to violate in a virgin as a vice?

"But alas! Destiny allows no dispute. Die, Hebe! Hebe, die! Woeful Hebe, and only accursed Hebe!

"Farewell, the sweet delights of life, and welcome now, the bitter pangs of death!

"Farewell, you chaste virgins, whose thoughts are divine, whose faces are fair, whose fortunes are agreeable with and correspond to your affections and desires!

"Enjoy, and long enjoy, the pleasure of your curled locks, the amiableness of your wished-for looks, the sweetness of your tuned voices, the content of your inward thoughts, the pomp and splendor of your outward appearances.

"Only Hebe bids farewell to all the joys that she conceived and imagined and that you hope for, that she possessed and that you shall possess.

"Farewell, the pomp of princes' courts, whose roofs are embossed with gold and whose pavements are decked with fair ladies; where the days are spent in sweet delights, and the nights are spent in pleasant dreams; where chastity honors affections and commands; and where chastity yields to desire and conquers!"

Chastity heightens sexual desire, and chaste marital sex triumphs over unchaste sexual desire.

Hebe continued:

"Farewell, the sovereign of all virtue and goddess of all virgins, Diana, whose perfections are impossible to be numbered and therefore infinite, never to be matched and therefore immortal!

"Farewell, sweet parents, yet, to be mine, unfortunate parents! How blessed would you have been in barrenness! How happy would I have been if I had not been born!

"Farewell, life, vain life, wretched life, whose sorrows are long, whose end is fearful, whose miseries are certain, whose hopes are innumerable, whose fears are intolerable!"

A proverb stated, "Long life has long misery."

Hebe continued:

"Come, Death, and welcome, Death, whom nature cannot resist, because necessity rules, nor can nature defer because destiny hastens!"

A proverb states, "As sure as death."

Another proverb states, "It is impossible to avoid (undo) fate (destiny)."

Hebe continued:

"Come, Agar, thou monster insatiable for maidens' blood and devourer of beauty's bowels. Glut thyself until thou surfeit, and let my life end thine. Tear these tender joints with thy greedy jaws, these yellow locks with thy black feet, this fair face with thy foul teeth.

"Why do thou abate and slacken thy accustomed swiftness? I am fair; I am a virgin; I am ready.

"Come, Agar, thou horrible monster, and farewell, world, thou viler monster!"

They waited, but no monster came.

The augur said, "The monster has not come, and therefore I see that Neptune is abused, disdained, and held in contempt, whose rage will, I fear, be both infinite and intolerable. Take in this virgin, whose lack of beauty has saved her own life and spoiled and destroyed all yours."

"We could not find any virgin fairer than she," Ericthinis, Hebe's father, said.

The augur said:

"Neptune will."

He then ordered the men:

"Go and deliver her to her father."

The men untied Hebe.

Hebe said:

"Fortunate Hebe, how shall thou express thy joys?

"Nay, unhappy girl, who are not the fairest. Wouldn't it have been better for thee to have died with fame and reputation than to live with dishonor, to have preferred the safety of thy country and the splendidness of thy beauty before the sweetness of life and the vanity of the world?

"But alas! Destiny would not have it so. Destiny could not, for it asks for and requires the most beautiful.

"I wish, Hebe, that thou had been the most beautiful."

Ericthinis, her father, said, "Come, Hebe, this is no time for us to reason and talk about this. It would have been best for us if thou had been most beautiful."

All exited.

Both still disguised, Phillida and Galatea talked together.

Phillida said, "We met the virgin who should have been offered to Neptune. Perhaps either the custom is pardoned or she is not thought the fairest and most beautiful."

"I cannot conjecture and surmise the cause, but I fear the outcome," Galatea said.

"Why should you fear the outcome?" Phillida said. "The god requires no boy as the sacrifice."

"I wish he did," Galatea said. "Then I would have no fear."

Phillida said:

"I am glad he does not, though, because if he did, I should have also cause to fear.

"But wait, what man or god is this? Let us secretly withdraw ourselves into the thickets."

The disguised Galatea and the disguised Phillida exited.

Alone, Neptune entered the scene.

Neptune said to himself:

"And do men begin to be equal with gods, seeking by crafty trickery to overreach and outwit them who by power oversee and govern them? Do they dote so much on their daughters that they do not hesitate to dally with our deities?

"The inhabitants shall well see that destiny cannot be prevented and forestalled by craft nor can my anger be appeased by submission. I will make havoc — widespread destruction — of Diana's nymphs. My temple shall be dyed with maidens' blood, and there shall be nothing viler than to be a virgin. To be young and fair shall be considered shame and punishment, insomuch as it shall be thought as dishonorable to be honest and chaste and inasmuch as it shall be thought fortunate to be deformed."

Diana and her nymphs entered the scene.

Diana, who had overheard Neptune, said, "O Neptune, have thou forgotten thyself, or will thou entirely forsake me? Has Diana therefore brought danger to her nymphs because they are chaste? Shall virtue suffer both pain and shame, which always deserves praise and honor?"

Venus entered the scene. She had been eavesdropping.

Venus said:

"Praise and honor, Neptune? Diana deserves nothing less, unless it is commendable to be disdainful and honorable to be peevish.

"Sweet Neptune, if Venus has any influence over you, let her try it in this one thing: that Diana may find as small comfort at thy hands as Love has found courtesy at hers. Diana is she who hates sweet delights, envies and is malicious toward loving desires, masks and covers wanton eyes, stops amorous ears, bridles and curbs youthful mouths, and, under a name or a word, that of 'constancy,' entertains and sanctions all kinds of cruelty.

"She has taken my son Cupid — Cupid, my lovely son — treating him like an apprentice, whipping him like a slave, scorning him like a beast. Therefore, Neptune, I entreat thee by no other god than the god of love that thou evilly treat this goddess of hate."

Neptune said:

"I muse not a little and am much perplexed to see you two in this place, at this time, and about this matter.

"But what do you say, Diana? Have you held Cupid captive?"

Diana said:

"I say there is nothing more in vain than to dispute with Venus, whose untamed affections have bred more brawls in heaven than is fit to repeat on earth or possible to recount in number.

"I have Cupid, and I will keep him — not to dandle and bounce him up and down in my lap, him whom I abhor in my heart, but to laugh to scorn him who has made in my virgins' hearts such deep scars."

Venus said:

"Diana, do you call them scars that I know to be bleeding wounds?

"Alas, weak deity! Your power does not stretch far enough both to abate the sharpness of his arrows and to heal the hurts.

"No, love's wounds, when they seem green and fresh, rankle and fester, and, having a smooth skin on the outside, they rankle and fester to the death within.

"Therefore, Neptune, if ever Venus stood thee in thy stead and did any service for you, if ever Venus furthered thy fancies and promoted thy desires, or if Venus shall at all times be at thy command, then let either Diana bring her virgins to a continual massacre or release Cupid from his martyrdom."

Neptune had many sex affairs, and Venus had been of assistance to him.

Diana said, "It is known, Venus, that your tongue is as unruly as your thoughts, and your thoughts as unstayed [wavering] and ungoverned and unstaid [not sober] as your eyes. Diana cannot chatter; Venus cannot choose to not chatter."

Venus said:

"It is an honor for Diana to have Venus mean ill, when she speaks so well."

She was sarcastic. Diana had been speaking ill about Venus.

Venus continued:

"But you shall see I did not come to trifle.

"Therefore, once again, Neptune, if that is not buried which can never die — amorous fancy — or if that is quenched which must forever burn — affection and desire — then show thyself the same Neptune that I knew thee to be when thou were a shepherd, and don't let Venus' words be in vain and without effect in thine ears, since thine words were imprinted in my heart."

Neptune said:

"It would be unfitting that goddesses should strive against each other, and it would be unreasonable that I should not yield.

"And therefore, to please both of you, both of you pay attention to my words. Diana I must honor; her virtue deserves no less. But Venus I must love; I must confess so much.

"Diana, restore Cupid to Venus, and I will forever release and stop the sacrifice of virgins. If therefore you love your nymphs as she loves her son, or if you do not rate a private grudge above a far-reaching grief, answer what you will do."

Diana had a private grudge with Cupid. The sacrifice of the virgins to Neptune affected many more people and so Neptune called it a far-reaching grief.

Diana said:

"I don't consider the choice hard, for if I had twenty Cupids, I would deliver them all to save one virgin, knowing love to be a thing of all the vainest and most futile, and virginity to be a virtue of all the noblest. I yield.

"Larissa, bring out Cupid."

Larissa exited.

Diana continued:

"And now it shall be said that Cupid saved those whom he thought to spoil and ruin."

Cupid had plagued the nymphs by making them fall in love, and now his role in this bargain ensued that beautiful, chaste virgins — another kind of nymph — would no longer be sacrificed.

Venus said, "I agree to this willingly, for I will be wary how my son wanders again. But Diana cannot forbid him to wound with his arrows."

"Yes, I can," Diana said. "Chastity is not within the level — the range — of his bow."

"But beauty is a fair mark to hit," Venus said. "It is both a legitimate target and an agreeable target."

Neptune said, "Well, I am glad you are in accord and are agreed, and that you say that Neptune has dealt well with beauty and chastity."

Venus and Diana were not entirely in accord, but Neptune was pretending that they were.

Larissa returned with Cupid.

Diana said to Venus, "Here, take your son."

Venus said to Cupid, "Sir boy, where have you been? Always taken, first by Sappho, now by Diana. How do such things happen, you unhappy and unfortunate elf?"

At the end of John Lyly's play *Sappho and Phao*, Cupid had rejected Venus and had stayed with Sappho.

Cupid said, "Coming through Diana's woods, and seeing so many fair faces with fond hearts, I thought for my entertainment to cause them pain by making them fall in love, and so I was taken by Diana."

"I am glad I have you," Venus said.

"And I am glad I am rid of him," Diana said.

Venus said to Cupid, "Alas, poor boy! Thy wings clipped? Thy torches quenched? Thy bow burnt? And thy arrows broken?"

"Aye, but it doesn't matter," Cupid said. "I bear now my arrows in my eyes, my wings on my thoughts, my torches in my ears, and my bow in my mouth, so that I can wound with looking, fly with thinking, burn with hearing, and shoot with speaking."

"Well, you shall go up to heaven with me, for on earth thou will lose me," Venus said.

Tityrus and Melebeus, the fathers of Galatea and Phillida, entered the scene.

Galatea and Phillida followed at a distance, unseen at first by the others.

"But wait, who are these men?" Neptune asked, seeing Tityrus and Melebeus.

"Those who have offended thee to save their daughters," Tityrus said.

Neptune asked Tityrus, "Why, did you have a fair daughter?"

"Aye, and Melebeus had a fair daughter," Tityrus said.

"Where are they?" Neptune asked.

"In yonder woods, and I think I see them coming," Melebeus said.

"Well, your deserts have not gotten you pardons, but these goddesses' jars — their quarrels — have gotten you pardons," Neptune said.

The two fathers' behavior had not gotten them a pardon, but the quarreling of Diana and Venus had gotten them a pardon.

"This is my daughter, my sweet Phillida," Melebeus said.

"And this is my fair Galatea," Tityrus said.

"Unfortunate is Galatea, if this is Phillida!" Galatea said.

"Accursed is Phillida, if that is Galatea!" Phillida said.

Galatea said to herself, "And were thou all this while enamored of and in love with Phillida, that sweet Phillida?"

Phillida said to herself, "And could thou dote upon the face of a maiden, thyself being one? Could thou dote on the face of fair Galatea?"

"Do you both, being maidens, love one another?" Neptune asked.

"I had thought the male clothing agreeable with and in accord with the male sex, and so I burned in the fire of my own fancies," Galatea said.

"I had thought that in the attire of a boy there could not have lodged the body of a virgin, and so I was inflamed with a sweet desire that now I find a sour deceit," Phillida said.

"Now things falling out as they do, you must leave these fond-found — now found to be foolish — affections. Nature will have it so; necessity must have it so," Diana said.

"I will never love any but Phillida," Galatea said. "Her love is engraved in my heart with her eyes."

"Nor will I love any but Galatea, whose faith is imprinted in my thoughts by her words," Phillida said.

Neptune said:

"An idle choice, strange and foolish, for one virgin to dote on another, and to imagine a constant faith where there can be no cause of affection.

"How do you like this, Venus?"

Venus said:

"I like it well, and I allow and approve it."

Venus! You go, girl!

Venus continued:

"They shall both be possessed of their wishes, for never shall it be said that Nature or Fortune shall overthrow Love and Faith and Loyalty."

Venus asked Galatea and Phillida, "Is your love unspotted, begun with truth, continued with constancy, and not to be altered until death?"

Galatea said, "Die, Galatea, if thy love is not so!"

Phillida said, "Accursed be thou, Phillida, if thy love is not so!"

"Suppose all this, Venus, what then?" Diana asked.

"Then it shall be seen that I can turn one of them into a man, and that I will," Venus said.

"Is it possible?" Diana said.

Venus replied:

"What is to Love or the mistress of love impossible? Wasn't it Venus who did the like to Iphis and Ianthes?"

Iphis and Ianthes were both born female, but Iphis was raised as a male. Her family was poor and unable to provide a dowry for her, and her mother feared that her husband would want the girl infant dead. The Egyptian goddess Isis visited the mother and told her to keep the baby's sex a secret and raise her as a boy. When Iphis was grown up, her father arranged a marriage for her with Ianthes: Both Iphis' father and Ianthes thought that Iphis was a male, and Ianthes fell in love with Iphis. In despair, Iphis' mother visited the temple of Isis and asked Isis for help. Isis responded by making Iphis a male. Iphis and Ianthe married and presumably lived happily together ever after, given that their wedding was presided over by Venus (goddess of sexual passion), Juno (goddess of marriage), and Hymen (god of marriage).

The story of Iphis and Ianthe is told in Ovid, *Metamorphoses*, Book 9.

Venus then asked Galatea and Phillida, "What do you say? Are you agreed that one of you will be made a boy immediately?"

"I am content, as long as I may embrace Galatea," Phillida said.

"Embrace." Nudge, nudge. Wink, wink.

"I wish it, as long as I may enjoy Phillida," Galatea said.

"Enjoy." Nudge, nudge. Wink, wink.

Melebeus said to Phillida, "Wait, daughter, you must know whether I will have you as a son."

Tityrus said to his daughter, "Don't forget about me and what I want, Galatea: I will keep you as I begat you, a daughter."

"Tityrus, let yours be a boy, and, if you will and if you like, mine shall not be a boy," Melebeus said.

"Nay, mine shall not, for by that means my young son shall lose his inheritance," Tityrus said.

Galatea was older than her brother; if Galatea became a man, her brother would lose his inheritance, which would go to the eldest son.

"Why then, get him made a maiden, and then there is nothing lost," Melebeus said.

"If there is to be such changing, I wish that Venus could make my wife change into a man," Tityrus said.

"Why?" Melebeus asked.

"Because she loves always to play with men," Tityrus said.

"Play" can mean "amuse herself." Such play may include sex.

"Well, you are both fond and foolish," Venus said. "Therefore, agree to this changing, or allow your daughters to endure hard misfortune and a bad fate."

"What do you say, Tityrus?" Melebeus asked. "Shall we refer it to Venus? Shall we let Venus decide?"

"I am content with that because she is a goddess," Tityrus said.

"Neptune, you will not dislike it?" Venus asked.

"Not I," Neptune said.

"Nor you, Diana?" Venus asked.

"Not I," Diana said.

"Cupid shall not," Venus said.

"I will not," Cupid agreed.

Venus said:

"Then let us depart. Neither of them shall know whose lot it shall be to become a boy until they come to the church door, where the marriage will be solemnized. One shall become a boy.

"Does this suffice? Does it satisfy you?"

Phillida said, "Yes, and it satisfies us both. Doesn't it, Galatea?"

"Yes, Phillida," Galatea said.

The brothers Rafe, Robin, and Dick entered the scene.

"Come, Robin, I am glad I have met with thee, for now we will make our father laugh at these tales," Rafe said.

"Who are these men who so malapertly and impudently thrust themselves into our companies?" Diana asked.

"Indeed, madam, we are 'fortune tellers,'" Robin said.

Venus said, "Fortune-tellers? Tell me my fortune. What is in my future?"

Rafe said, "We do not mean fortune-tellers, we mean 'fortune tellers': tellers of our fortunes and our luck. We can tell what fortune we have had these twelve months in the woods."

"Let them alone," Diana said. "Ignore them. They are only peevish: foolish and perverse."

"Yet they will be as good as minstrels at the marriage, to make us all merry," Venus said.

"Aye, ladies, we bear a very good consort: a very good harmony," Dick said.

Venus asked Rafe, "Can you sing?"

Rafe replied, "Basely."

Venus asked Dick, "And can you sing?"

Dick said, "Meanly."

Venus asked Robin, "And what can you do?"

Robin said, "If they double it, I will treble it."

The three brothers could sing bass, tenor (the mean between bass and treble), and treble — but perhaps not very well.

A song with two singers is doubled; with three, it is trebled.

Venus said, "Then all of you shall go with us, and sing the nuptial hymn 'Hymen' before the marriage. Are you content? Are you happy with this?"

Rafe said, "Content? Never better content for our bellies! For there we shall be sure to fill our bellies with capons' rumps, or some such dainty dishes."

A capon is a castrated cock.

Then follow us," Venus said.

EPILOGUE

Galatea stepped forward.

She said to the others:

"Go, all of you. It is only I who shall conclude all."

The others exited.

Galatea then said to the ladies reading this book:

"You ladies may see that Venus can make constancy fickleness, Venus can make courage cowardice, and Venus can make modesty lightness, working things impossible in your sex and tempering hardest hearts like softest wool.

"Yield, ladies, yield to love, ladies, which lurks under your eyelids while you sleep and plays with your heartstrings while you wake; whose sweetness never breeds satiety, whose labor never breeds weariness, and whose grief never breeds bitterness.

"Cupid was begotten in a mist, nursed in clouds, and suckled only upon conceits and fancies.

"Confess that he is a conqueror whom you ought to regard with respect, since it is impossible to resist him; for this is infallible, that love conquers all things but itself, and ladies conquer all hearts but their own."

Question: Are the male readers of this book honorary ladies?

Of course.

— NOTES —

— 1.4 —

For Your Information: Erotic asphyxiation:

Do male prisoners have an erection and ejaculate during hanging?

In popular culture it has often been claimed that men have erections and ejaculate when hanged.

Some refer to this as "angel lust".

So do these things actually happen? The answer appears to be YES to both, but very rarely.

Source: "Some myths and facts surrounding execution by hanging." 9 October 2013
http://www.capitalpunishmentuk.org/Hanging_myths.pdf

— 2.3 —

PETER

A little more than a man, and a hair's breadth less than
a god. He can make of thy cap gold, and, by multiplica-
tion of one groat, he can make three old angels.
(2.3.43-45)
Source of Above: Lyly, John. *Galatea* and *Midas*. *Galatea* edited by George K. Hunter. *Midas* edited by David Bevington. The Revels Plays. New York: St. Martin's Press, 2000. Page 53.

For Your Information: The Great Debasement

The Great Debasement (1544–1551) was a currency debasement policy introduced in 1544 England under the order of Henry VIII which saw the amount of precious metal in gold and silver coins reduced and in some cases replaced entirely with cheaper base metals such as copper. Overspending by Henry VIII to pay for his lavish lifestyle and to fund foreign wars with France and Scotland are cited as reasons for the policy's introduction. The main aim of the policy was to increase revenue for the Crown at the cost of taxpayers through savings in currency production with less bullion being required to mint new coins. During debasement gold standards dropped from the previous standard of 23 karat to as low as 20 karat while silver was reduced from 92.5% sterling silver to just 25%. Revoked in 1551 by Edward VI, the policy's economic effects continued for many years until 1560 when all debased currency was removed from circulation.

Source: "The Great Debasement." Wikipedia. Accessed 18 November 2022.

https://en.wikipedia.org/wiki/The_Great_Debasement

PETER

The third, [third spirit is] sal ammoniac.

RAFE

A proper word.

(2.3-63-64)

Source of Above: Lyly, John. *Galatea* and *Midas*. *Galatea* edited by George K. Hunter. *Midas* edited by David Bevington. The Revels Plays. New York: St. Martin's Press, 2000. Page 54.

George K. Hunter suggested that Rafe may have been thinking of "demoniac," given that the conversation is about spirits.

What follows are David Bruce's speculations about "sal ammoniac."

Salam or *Salaam* is an Arabic word that means "peace" and is used as a greeting. The Hebrew word for "peace" is *shalom*.

Perhaps "sal ammoniac" means "*Salam*, demoniac" and is an incantation to greet a person possessed by a demon.

In the *Oxford English Dictionary*, the first citation for *salaam* as a noun is 1613, and as a verb is 1684.

***

In 1 Samuel 11, King Saul wins a battle over the King Nahash and the Ammonites. King Nahash of Ammon was an evil man who threatened Israel, and the country of Ammon was a hostile neighbor to Israel. The Israelites may have regarded King Nahash as possessed by a demon.

The suffix *-iac* can indicate a sufferer from a disease. If King Nahash is a demoniac, then he suffers from being possessed by a demon: a disease that can be cured by exorcism.

King Nahash was sinful. If sin can be regarded as a disease, King Nahash of Ammon was afflicted by a disease.

In the tenth ditch of the eighth circle of Dante's *Inferno*, the falsifiers are afflicted by disease. The alchemists have leprosy (the alchemists tried to change lead into gold, and now their skin turns from healthy to diseased). The evil impersonators are insane (the evil impersonators made other people confused about who the evil impersonators were; now the evil impersonators, who are insane, are confused about who they are). The counterfeiters — who made what they had bigger than it should be — have dropsy, aka edema (which makes part of their body swell up and be bigger than it should be). The liars — whose testimony stank — are feverous and stink.

King Nahash wanted the people of Jabesh-Gilead to submit to him. If they did, he would spare their lives but blind their right eye. The people of Jabesh-Gilead sent messengers throughout Israel to ask for help, and Saul, who was then a herdsman and not yet King of Israel and who was angry at the Ammonites, quickly gathered soldiers and defeated the Ammonites in battle.

"Sal ammoniac" may mean "Saul, whom the country of Ammon made sick with anger."

Also, Saul's anger was righteous anger, and he may have been filled with the Holy Spirit.

***

Of course, I thought of Salem, but the Salem Witch Trial occurred a century later in 1692-1693. *Galatea* was first published in 1592.

PETER

Didst thou never hear how Jupiter came in a golden
shower to Danae?
(2.3.98-99)
Source of Above: Lyly, John. *Galatea* and *Midas*. *Galatea* edited by George K. Hunter. *Midas* edited by David Bevington. The Revels Plays. New York: St. Martin's Press, 2000. Page 56.

For Your Information: From Apollodorus, *Library* 2.4:

When Acrisius inquired of the oracle how he should get male children, the god said that his daughter would give birth to a son who would kill him. Fearing that, Acrisius built a brazen chamber under ground and there guarded Danae. However, she was seduced, as some say, by Proetus, whence arose the quarrel between them; but some say that Zeus had intercourse with her in the shape of a stream of gold which poured through the roof into Danae's lap. When Acrisius afterwards learned that she had got a child Perseus, he would not believe that she had been seduced by Zeus, and putting his daughter with the child in a chest, he cast it into the sea. The chest was washed ashore on Seriphus, and Dictys took up the boy and reared him.

Source:
Apollodorus, *Library*. Sir James George Frazer, Ed. Perseus. Accessed 18 November 2022.

http://www.perseus.tufts.edu/hopper/
text?doc=Perseus:text:1999.01.0022:text=Library:book=2:chapter=4

— 3.1 —

EUROTA

> *Telusa, Diana told me to hunt you out, and she said that you*
> *don't care to hunt with her; but if you follow any other*
> *game than the game she has roused, your punishment shall be to*
> *bend all our bows and weave all our strings.*

(3.1.31-34)

Source of Above: Lyly, John. *Galatea* and *Midas*. *Galatea* edited by George K. Hunter. *Midas* edited by David Bevington. The Revels Plays. New York: St. Martin's Press, 2000. Page 61.

For Your Information:

The bowstring

Although manufactured bowstrings are available, some archery enthusiasts prefer to make their own.

The number of strands of thread needed is determined. This depends on the strength of the thread being used and the draw weight (strength) of the bow. The bundle of strands is divided into three equal sets, and each set is coated with beeswax (perhaps with added resin). The sets of strands are then formed into a cord by twisting and weaving them together.

Source: "Bow and Arrow." How Things are Made." Accessed 18 November 2022.

http://www.madehow.com/Volume-5/
Bow-and-Arrow.html#ixzz7l1jHeHZQ

For Your Information:

Medieval bowstrings were most commonly made of hemp, a plant fiber that was relatively available, strong, and resistant. Flax was also sometimes used, as was (on occasion) silk. For average people,

93

bowstrings may also be made of animal sinews or other cheap plant fibers.

Source: "What Were Medieval Bow Strings Made Of?" Study.com. Accessed 18 November 2022.
https://homework.study.com/explanation/what-were-medieval-bow-strings-made-of.html

— 3.3 —

ASTRONOMER

> *I can tell thee*
> *what weather shall be between this moment and* octogessimus octavus
> mirabilis annus.
> (3.3.43-45)

Source of Above: Lyly, John. *Galatea* and *Midas*. *Galatea* edited by George K. Hunter. *Midas* edited by David Bevington. The Revels Plays. New York: St. Martin's Press, 2000. Page 71.

For Your Information:

The biggest media event of the sixteenth century occurred in 1523-24, when scores of astrologers jumped onto a bandwagon of collective hysteria by proclaiming the imminent end of the world. The final days, the astrologers announced, would occur as a result of a second Deluge brought on by a conjunction of the three upper planets, Jupiter, Saturn, and Mars, in the sign of Pisces.

[...]

The European fascination with the Wonder Year of 1588 can be traced back to the supposed discovery among the papers of the German astronomer Regiomontanus (Johannes Müller) of a doggerel verse predicting great calamities for that year, which he was alleged to have scribbled on a leaf of paper.

[...]

As in 1524, the annus mirabilis *came and went without calamitous results—much less the Second Coming. Astrologers, who had gone out on a limb predicting the end of the world, became the butt of ridicule. Philip Stubbes, in his* Anatomy of Abuses *(1583) chided the "foolish star tooters," whose "presumptuous audacity and rash boldness ...*

brought the world into such wonderful perplexity." Henry Howard,
Earl of Northampton, wrote that the astrologers should be shunned
"like a dragon's den.["]

Source: William Eamon, "Astrology and Prophecy in the Renaissance." 20 November 2011

https://williameamon.com/astrology-and-prophecy-in-the-renaissance/

— 5.3 —

At the end of the play, either Galatea or Phillida will become a boy, aka a transgender man. All indications are that the two will live happily ever after. (Some important gods attend the wedding, and it is clear that Galatea and Phillida love each other.) More power to them.

For Your Information:

In 1949, journalist James Morris married Elizabeth Tuckniss. Later, Mr. Morris got a sex change and became Jan Morris. Because of the sex change, the married couple was forced to divorce, but they continued to live together. In 2008, in a civil service ceremony, Jan Morris, now a writer, re-married Elizabeth Tuckniss. Ms. Morris pointed out, "I have lived with the same person for 58 years. We were married when I was young ... and then this sex-change, so-called, happened, so we naturally had to divorce ... but we always lived together, anyway. So, I wanted to round this thing off nicely. So last week, as a matter of fact, Elizabeth and I went and had a civil union." Ms. Tuckniss says, "After Jan had a sex change, we had to divorce. So there we were. It did not make any difference to me. We still had our family. We just carried on."

Why do some marriages endure that seem unlikely to endure?

British journalist Stuart Jeffries says, "You know what — it's none of our business. ... Enough that some mysteries remain just that."

Source: Stuart Jeffries, "Unlikely in love — couples who beat the odds." *The Guardian.* 5 June 2008 <http://www.guardian.co.uk/world/2008/jun/05/gayrights.relationships>.

The anecdote was retold in David Bruce's own words, and it appears in his book *The Funniest People in Families, Volume 6: 250 Anecdotes*:

https://www.smashwords.com/books/view/108857

APPENDIX A: FAIR USE

§ 107. Limitations on exclusive rights: Fair use

Release date: 2004-04-30

Notwithstanding the provisions of sections 106 and 106A, the fair use of a copyrighted work, including such use by reproduction in copies or phonorecords or by any other means specified by that section, for purposes such as criticism, comment, news reporting, teaching (including multiple copies for classroom use), scholarship, or research, is not an infringement of copyright. In determining whether the use made of a work in any particular case is a fair use the factors to be considered shall include —

(1) the purpose and character of the use, including whether such use is of a commercial nature or is for nonprofit educational purposes;

(2) the nature of the copyrighted work;

(3) the amount and substantiality of the portion used in relation to the copyrighted work as a whole; and

(4) the effect of the use upon the potential market for or value of the copyrighted work.

The fact that a work is unpublished shall not itself bar a finding of fair use if such finding is made upon consideration of all the above factors.

Source of Fair Use information:

http://www.law.cornell.edu/uscode/17/107.html

APPENDIX B: ABOUT THE AUTHOR

It was a dark and stormy night. Suddenly a cry rang out, and on a hot summer night in 1954, Josephine, wife of Carl Bruce, gave birth to a boy — me. Unfortunately, this young married couple allowed Reuben Saturday, Josephine's brother, to name their first-born. Reuben, aka "The Joker," decided that Bruce was a nice name, so he decided to name me Bruce Bruce. I have gone by my middle name — David — ever since.

Being named Bruce David Bruce hasn't been all bad. Bank tellers remember me very quickly, so I don't often have to show an ID. It can be fun in charades, also. When I was a counselor as a teenager at Camp Echoing Hills in Warsaw, Ohio, a fellow counselor gave the signs for "sounds like" and "two words," then she pointed to a bruise on her leg twice. Bruise Bruise? Oh yeah, Bruce Bruce is the answer!

Uncle Reuben, by the way, gave me a haircut when I was in kindergarten. He cut my hair short and shaved a small bald spot on the back of my head. My mother wouldn't let me go to school until the bald spot grew out again.

Of all my brothers and sisters (six in all), I am the only transplant to Athens, Ohio. I was born in Newark, Ohio, and have lived all around Southeastern Ohio. However, I moved to Athens to go to Ohio University and have never left.

At Ohio U, I never could make up my mind whether to major in English or Philosophy, so I got a bachelor's degree with a double major in both areas, then I added a Master of Arts degree in English and a Master of Arts degree in Philosophy. Yes, I have my MAMA degree.

Currently, and for a long time to come (I eat fruits and veggies), I am spending my retirement writing books such as *Nadia Comaneci: Perfect 10*, *The Funniest People in Comedy*, *Homer's* Iliad: *A Retelling in Prose*, and *William Shakespeare's* Hamlet: *A Retelling in Prose*.

If all goes well, I will publish one or two books a year for the rest of my life. (On the other hand, a good way to make God laugh is to tell Her your plans.)

By the way, my sister Brenda Kennedy writes romances such as *A New Beginning* and *Shattered Dreams*.

APPENDIX C: SOME BOOKS BY DAVID BRUCE

Retellings of a Classic Work of Literature

Arden of Faversham: *A Retelling*

Ben Jonson's The Alchemist: *A Retelling*

Ben Jonson's The Arraignment, or Poetaster: *A Retelling*

Ben Jonson's Bartholomew Fair: *A Retelling*

Ben Jonson's The Case is Altered: *A Retelling*

Ben Jonson's Catiline's Conspiracy: *A Retelling*

Ben Jonson's The Devil is an Ass: *A Retelling*

Ben Jonson's Epicene: *A Retelling*

Ben Jonson's Every Man in His Humor: *A Retelling*

Ben Jonson's Every Man Out of His Humor: *A Retelling*

Ben Jonson's The Fountain of Self-Love, or Cynthia's Revels: *A Retelling*

Ben Jonson's The Magnetic Lady, or Humors Reconciled: *A Retelling*

Ben Jonson's The New Inn, or The Light Heart: *A Retelling*

Ben Jonson's Sejanus' Fall: *A Retelling*

Ben Jonson's The Staple of News: *A Retelling*

Ben Jonson's A Tale of a Tub: *A Retelling*

Ben Jonson's Volpone, or the Fox: *A Retelling*

Christopher Marlowe's Complete Plays: Retellings

Christopher Marlowe's Dido, Queen of Carthage: *A Retelling*

Christopher Marlowe's Doctor Faustus: *Retellings of the 1604 A-Text and of the 1616 B-Text*

Christopher Marlowe's Edward II: *A Retelling*

Christopher Marlowe's The Massacre at Paris: *A Retelling*

Christopher Marlowe's The Rich Jew of Malta: *A Retelling*

Christopher Marlowe's Tamburlaine, Parts 1 and 2: *Retellings*

Dante's Divine Comedy: *A Retelling in Prose*

Dante's Inferno: *A Retelling in Prose*

Dante's Purgatory: *A Retelling in Prose*

Dante's Paradise: *A Retelling in Prose*

The Famous Victories of Henry V: *A Retelling*

From the Iliad *to the* Odyssey: *A Retelling in Prose of Quintus of Smyrna's* Posthomerica

George Chapman, Ben Jonson, and John Marston's Eastward Ho! *A Retelling*

George Peele's The Arraignment of Paris: *A Retelling*

George Peele's The Battle of Alcazar: *A Retelling*

George's Peele's David and Bathsheba, and the Tragedy of Absalom: *A Retelling*

George Peele's Edward I: *A Retelling*

George Peele's The Old Wives' Tale: *A Retelling*

George-a-Greene: *A Retelling*

The History of King Leir: *A Retelling*

Homer's Iliad: *A Retelling in Prose*

Homer's Odyssey: *A Retelling in Prose*

J.W. Gent.'s The Valiant Scot: *A Retelling*

Jason and the Argonauts: A Retelling in Prose of Apollonius of Rhodes' Argonautica

John Ford: Eight Plays Translated into Modern English

John Ford's The Broken Heart: *A Retelling*

John Ford's The Fancies, Chaste and Noble: *A Retelling*

John Ford's The Lady's Trial: *A Retelling*

John Ford's The Lover's Melancholy: *A Retelling*

John Ford's Love's Sacrifice: *A Retelling*

John Ford's Perkin Warbeck: *A Retelling*

John Ford's The Queen: *A Retelling*

John Ford's 'Tis Pity She's a Whore: *A Retelling*

John Lyly's Campaspe: *A Retelling*

John Lyly's Endymion, The Man in the Moon: *A Retelling*

John Lyly's Galatea: *A Retelling*

John Lyly's Love's Metamorphosis: *A Retelling*

John Lyly's Midas: *A Retelling*

John Lyly's Mother Bombie: *A Retelling*

John Lyly's Sappho and Phao: *A Retelling*

John Lyly's The Woman in the Moon: *A Retelling*

John Webster's The White Devil: *A Retelling*

King Edward III: *A Retelling*

Mankind: *A Medieval Morality Play* (A Retelling)

Margaret Cavendish's The Unnatural Tragedy: *A Retelling*

The Merry Devil of Edmonton: *A Retelling*

The Summoning of Everyman: *A Medieval Morality Play* (A Retelling)

Robert Greene's Friar Bacon and Friar Bungay: *A Retelling*

The Taming of a Shrew: *A Retelling*

Tarlton's Jests: A Retelling

Thomas Middleton's A Chaste Maid in Cheapside: *A Retelling*

Thomas Middleton's Women Beware Women: *A Retelling*

Thomas Middleton and Thomas Dekker's The Roaring Girl: *A Retelling*

Thomas Middleton and William Rowley's The Changeling: *A Retelling*

The Trojan War and Its Aftermath: Four Ancient Epic Poems

Virgil's Aeneid: *A Retelling in Prose*

William Shakespeare's 5 Late Romances: Retellings in Prose

William Shakespeare's 10 Histories: Retellings in Prose

William Shakespeare's 11 Tragedies: Retellings in Prose

William Shakespeare's 12 Comedies: Retellings in Prose

William Shakespeare's 38 Plays: Retellings in Prose

William Shakespeare's 1 Henry IV, aka Henry IV, Part 1: *A Retelling in Prose*

William Shakespeare's 2 Henry IV, aka Henry IV, Part 2: *A Retelling in Prose*

William Shakespeare's 1 Henry VI, aka Henry VI, Part 1: *A Retelling in Prose*

William Shakespeare's 2 Henry VI, aka Henry VI, Part 2: *A Retelling in Prose*

William Shakespeare's 3 Henry VI, aka Henry VI, Part 3: *A Retelling in Prose*

William Shakespeare's All's Well that Ends Well: *A Retelling in Prose*

William Shakespeare's Antony and Cleopatra: *A Retelling in Prose*

William Shakespeare's As You Like It: *A Retelling in Prose*

William Shakespeare's The Comedy of Errors: *A Retelling in Prose*

William Shakespeare's Coriolanus: *A Retelling in Prose*

William Shakespeare's Cymbeline: *A Retelling in Prose*

William Shakespeare's Hamlet: *A Retelling in Prose*

William Shakespeare's Henry V: *A Retelling in Prose*

William Shakespeare's Henry VIII: *A Retelling in Prose*

William Shakespeare's Julius Caesar: *A Retelling in Prose*

William Shakespeare's King John: *A Retelling in Prose*

William Shakespeare's King Lear: *A Retelling in Prose*

William Shakespeare's Love's Labor's Lost: *A Retelling in Prose*

William Shakespeare's Macbeth: *A Retelling in Prose*

William Shakespeare's Measure for Measure: *A Retelling in Prose*

William Shakespeare's The Merchant of Venice: *A Retelling in Prose*

William Shakespeare's The Merry Wives of Windsor: *A Retelling in Prose*

William Shakespeare's A Midsummer Night's Dream: *A Retelling in Prose*

William Shakespeare's Much Ado About Nothing: *A Retelling in Prose*

William Shakespeare's Othello: *A Retelling in Prose*

William Shakespeare's Pericles, Prince of Tyre: *A Retelling in Prose*

William Shakespeare's Richard II: *A Retelling in Prose*

William Shakespeare's Richard III: *A Retelling in Prose*

William Shakespeare's Romeo and Juliet: *A Retelling in Prose*

William Shakespeare's The Taming of the Shrew: *A Retelling in Prose*

William Shakespeare's The Tempest: *A Retelling in Prose*

William Shakespeare's Timon of Athens: *A Retelling in Prose*

William Shakespeare's Titus Andronicus: *A Retelling in Prose*

William Shakespeare's Troilus and Cressida: *A Retelling in Prose*

William Shakespeare's Twelfth Night: *A Retelling in Prose*

William Shakespeare's The Two Gentlemen of Verona: *A Retelling in Prose*

William Shakespeare's The Two Noble Kinsmen: *A Retelling in Prose*

William Shakespeare's The Winter's Tale: *A Retelling in Prose*

www.ingramcontent.com/pod-product-compliance
Lightning Source LLC
Chambersburg PA
CBHW051229160726
47994CB00002B/810

9798215357934